She wavered a bit, but spoke strongly. "Any chance you could move the baby seat over to Marisel's car? It's that green Forrester across the street."

Emilio, whose gaze had stayed on the door where Marisel had disappeared, looked at Cooper. "I'm on it."

Soon Marisel was back and Emilio helped the group get settled in the station wagon. Cooper turned to Sylvia. Her gaze followed the car as the rain and dark engulfed it.

"They named the baby Aniya. It means, look up to God."

He was quiet for a moment, watching her. The urgent need to act that had driven her for the last half-hour was gone now. She looked about to collapse.

He bit down on the urge to comfort. His fingers itched to take her arms and snug her up against his chest. He reminded himself of his job. "Did you get a look at the car the shooter was in?"

Instead of answering, she bent over, leaning with her hands on her thighs, her head down.

Cooper took her arms and raised her back up. "Are you okay?"

Her only response was a soft moan as she swayed a bit on her feet. He steadied her and she looked up at him. Without taking her gaze from his, she slowly slid one hand under her jacket. When she brought it back out, she held it between them, palm up. Cooper looked down and saw it was covered with blood.

"Shit." He grabbed her wrist. "Is that yours?"

She didn't answer, didn't take her eyes from his face. Cooper brushed her jacket aside and saw her white tee shirt was soaked with blood, from her ribs all the way down her right side. The black stain, glimmering crimson in the limited light, seeped into the jeans she wore.

"Baby," he said, not stopping to think about how improper that was. He took her up into his arms and looked around. The ambulance was gone. He carried her to the squad car, cursing himself for failing to take the basic step of ascertaining the number of injured. Where had he left his head?

"Emilio!" He called his partner over. "She's been hit. Get Jackson over here to drive us in." He slid into the rear seat, keeping her held tight in his arms. Soon Jackson was in the driver's seat, cranking the engine. Emilio held the back door open for a moment, giving Cooper a look.

Cooper met it, but had no explanation to give. "Oh, yeah—I think there's another woman in labor up there. You'd better stay with her until someone else gets here."

Emilio paled.

"Don't worry. She's only three centimeters—she's got some time yet." Now there was a little green around the edges of pale. "Help's coming."

Emilio seemed frozen, so Cooper pulled the door shut himself. "Let's go."

Tires squealed as they pulled out. Acceleration pressed him back into the seat and brought Sylvia's weight harder against his chest. He brushed strands of wet hair away from her face, stroking. Her eyes opened and he kissed her forehead, then tucked her head against his shoulder.

"I couldn't see the color of the car. It was dark. They didn't have their lights on."

"Shh." He kept his lips on her forehead, wondering at but accepting the pounding of his heart.

"The gun came out of the back window. It was rolled down, but not all the way, like one of those cars where the back window only opens half-way."

He shushed her again, biting back the word that was in his head—sweetheart. He enforced it this time by putting his lips to hers. When he lifted his face to look at her, she was watching him.

"Investigator—"

"Cooper."

"Cooper. You kissed me."

"Yes." He wanted more. He wanted to loosen her hair and bury his hands in it. He wanted the taste of her, the feel of her. He wanted her safe.

He squeezed gently where his hand held her against him. "Hush, please. Rest."

"I was shot, wasn't I?"

He nodded, fighting icy fingers of fear that nearly stopped his breath. He stroked her face as he felt the wetness of her blood saturate the leg of his jeans. He hardly knew her, but he wasn't sure he would survive losing her.

He could barely hear when she echoed his thoughts.

"What a strange night."

JYNIE'S PLACE

Rebecca Skovgaard

Whimsical Publications, LLC

Florida

ACKNOWLEDGEMENTS

To Anthony, Aleksandr, Ulysses, and Eleanor. Thank you for always supporting me and for frequently making me laugh. Maybe you think you know how much you mean to me. You're probably wrong.

CHAPTER ONE

"Great job, Nicci. Stay with it. You're almost done." Sylvia Huston spoke softly, encouraging.

Danniqwa rested, awaiting the next, nearly last, contraction.

The baby's father, Alejandro, slipped an ice chip into her mouth and followed it with a gentle kiss to her forehead. "You're so beautiful, baby."

The midwife sat back, quiet now, not wishing to intrude on this intimate moment. They were a remarkable couple. Nicci had the face of an African princess and a lithe dancer's body. She'd kept her place in a nationally recognized dance troupe until the sixth month of her pregnancy.

Alejandro was a handsome Latino, a graduate student at University of Rochester's Hochstein School of Music. They'd met at the School of the Arts when they were seventeen. Both came from the inner city, where drugs and gang violence robbed the future from many of their peers. Gifted with determination and natural talent, mentored by adults who recognized their potential, these two had found another path.

Part of that path, their love for each other, brought them to this moment.

It brought them here alone. Danniqwa and Alejandro's love had crossed lines of race, divisions of family and neighborhood loyalty. For this baby, there were no anxious grandmothers peeking into the birth room, no young cousins being entertained in the family room downstairs, no soon-to-be uncles snoring on the couch. Neither family had forgiven the betrayal.

With quiet strength, Nicci gave a weary smile. She kept eye contact with Alejandro as the next contraction rose. She bore down, using her strong abdominals and the control of breath that came with her training.

She pushed. The baby's head slid into view, all glistening

black curls.

Sylvia smiled. "Look, Alejandro, that's your daughter. Nicci, do you want to touch your baby's head?"

Quietly, Marisel Soto, Sylvia's birth assistant, slipped into the room. She clicked on the heating pad that warmed a stack of baby blankets then checked the emergency equipment that was always ready but seldom used. Tasks done, she rested an encouraging hand on Alejandro's shoulder.

"It's coming!" For the first time, panic tightened Nicci's voice.

"Yes. Let it come. Don't be afraid." The litany of reassurance continued. The baby crowned. Three pairs of hands, Sylvia's gloved and skilled, Nicci's and Alejandro's warm and loving, welcomed baby Aniya into the world.

Sylvia placed the baby on Nicci's abdomen while the new mother lay back to catch her breath, hands cradling her newborn. Alejandro unashamedly wiped tears on the sleeve of his tee shirt, alternately praising Nicci and admiring their new daughter.

Sylvia shared a satisfied smile with Marisel. A sharp October wind slapped cold rain against the window, reminding her of the harsh world this little family faced. She worried over them. But here, in this room, they were warm and safe. She'd given them the best start she could.

Gently, she dried the baby with the warm blankets and then checked the cord. When it stopped pulsating, Sylvia clamped it and handed the scissors to Alejandro. Using the couple's camera, Marisel took the picture as Aniya became her own girl.

✦ ✸ ✦

"There's report of a shooting on the 4700 block of Rosedale Ave. Police and ambulance requested." It was the scratchy voice of the Rochester PD dispatcher.

"Damn it!" Cooper Billings's heartfelt curse was punctuated by his partner's fist pounding hard once against the steering wheel. Emilio punched it. Their unmarked car fishtailed on the wet, nearly icy pavement as he took a corner hard.

Cooper slapped the flashing light onto the dash and reached for the radio. "Navarre and Billings, responding."

Emilio screeched the sedan to a stop in the middle of the next intersection. They searched in all directions and this time they both cursed. The streets were empty—no taillights to follow, no car slinking away with a shooter hurriedly secreting his gun under the backseat.

They'd been so close Cooper could nearly taste it. Their best source had sent them out on this nasty, rainy night. There would be a shooting, he said, at the birth center located on Rosedale. If they'd been just three minutes faster, they'd have seen it, maybe stopped it.

Instead, they'd have to deal with the aftermath.

Eyes scanning, Cooper took in the scene as Emilio pulled the sedan to the curb. What had happened was done. The victim lay on the sidewalk in a pool of his own blood. On the steps a young woman cried. She rocked, comforting herself and the bundle she cradled at her breast.

He had to assume the bundle contained a baby. The birth center, Tynie's Place, had opened about three years ago. Cooper knew little about it, only that many women in the neighborhood had their babies there.

He figured that was a lucky thing for the victim, because the woman giving first aid looked like she knew what she was doing. A second woman had her arms around the girl on the steps, using her body to block the view of the bleeding young man. Whether she was family or birth center staff, he didn't have a clue.

Cooper widened his visual search of the area. Wet leaves, vivid gold and orange fading now to flat brown, littered the walks and front porches. Rain slashed down like confetti in the flashing blue light. The freezing wind off Lake Ontario turned it to icy needles. The street and sidewalks were empty. None of the neighbors lifted a blind or pulled aside a curtain to see what was happening. In this neighborhood, everyone stayed away from the windows when gunshots pierced the night.

"Looks clear," he murmured. Emilio had already called in to confirm the need for an ambulance. He nodded and they both opened their doors.

Cooper touched the silver cross that hung at his neck then stepped out of the car. He reached to his side to loosen the safety strap on his holster but left the gun where it was. "Police," he called out. "Everyone stay where you are."

He couldn't see that he'd made much of an impression. He took the few steps to the victim and the woman kneeling over him. She was in her late twenties, probably taller than average for a woman. Her hair was haphazardly held back in one of those prongy barrettes that always looked slightly dangerous to him. The long strands were brown and dull, now, darkened with rain. He guessed that was deceiving, that there would be a rich, golden glow to it when it was dry.

Cooper didn't pause to consider whether that thought constituted a bit more than professional assessment of a potential witness. "Police, ma'am. Investigator Billings. What happened here?"

He knelt across from her, cold wet seeping quickly through his jeans. He could smell the blood and the fear of the young man between them. The victim's breath was labored and quick, panicky.

The woman made soothing noises to the man lying on the walk. She touched him gently, reassuring. Cooper watched her hands for a moment. Warm and strong, he thought, and without rings.

She'd used a baby blanket to put pressure against the wound. She lifted it now to check the bleeding.

He gave up waiting for her response. He patted his hands down the victim's body. He was mildly surprised when he didn't find any weapons.

And significantly surprised when the woman slapped his hands away. He shot her a hard look. Blue eyes flashed back. "He was here for the birth of his daughter." Grief and anger warred in her voice, roughening it. "He wasn't out here scoring drugs or looking for his gang rivals."

Cooper leashed his own anger only a little. He was a cop, doing his job, and nobody slapped at him for it. "Looks like they found him, though, doesn't it?"

"Yes." Bitter fury lined her face. She slashed at her tears with the cuff of her jacket. "You're here now. Why couldn't you have been here five minutes ago?"

He already had that burden of frustration and failure. He didn't need pretty blue eyes swimming in tears, too. His jaw clenched as he reined in some other emotion, different than his anger. Whatever it was, she seemed to know it was there. Her face softened and for a moment she lifted her hand, as though to touch him.

Sudden quiet broke the spell. A beat up old Tercel had been left running at the curb. Cooper had caught sight of the baby car seat strapped into the back as he'd walked past it. He looked up now to see that Emilio had reached in to shut off the ignition. Emilio held his gaze as he walked around the car then approached the pair on the steps.

The woman had turned her attention back to her patient. Cooper saw the rain slide down her neck, under her jacket that hung open. He knew it was only adrenaline that kept her from shivering with cold. "An ambulance is on the way. I want you to tell me what you saw here."

She spared him a quick glance. "I'm sorry. I will, soon." She looked over to the steps and called out. "Marisel! I need an IV set-up, and a couple bags of LR. Fast. And some blankets."

The woman on the stairs nodded. "*Si*, Sylvia." She was Hispanic, mid-thirties, Cooper thought, and very pretty with long, gently curling hair. She gave the girl a squeeze, shot a warning look to Emilio, and then hurried up the steps.

Taking her place at the girl's side, Emilio began speaking to her in a soft, comforting voice. As often happened, the young woman quieted, responding to his gentleness. She looked at Emilio for a moment, tears trailing down her elegant cheeks, then buried her face against the baby in her arms.

Cooper looked back at the woman across from him. "You a doctor, Sylvia?"

She lifted her eyes again from the victim, annoyance at the interruption showing. "I'm..." Her eyes searched his as she paused.

He felt her puzzlement, saw her eyes narrow before she shook herself.

"I'm a midwife." Her voice was like Irish Cream, whiskey-flavored, sweet. "I need light. Do you have a flashlight?"

Her attention was gone; he was aware of its absence. She tore at the victim's sleeve, pulled it up to bare his arm. She wrapped her hand around the arm just below the elbow and squeezed. A mild curse passed her lips.

She ignored him as the other woman returned with supplies. Marisel opened the IV bag and ran fluid through the tubing while Sylvia placed a tourniquet and looked again for a vein. She gave Cooper a short, sharp glance, clearly won-

dering why he was still there. *"Light,"* she said, with no uncertain emphasis. "Get me a flashlight."

Cooper bowed to her authority with only a small spasm of
resistance. He got the flashlight from the unmarked and
shone it down where she was working. She nodded her satisfaction then threaded a needle into a vein he would have
sworn wasn't there.

Marisel opened the clamp; fluid began to drip. "Hold this
up high," she instructed, handing him the bag and moving
back to the woman on the steps. Cooper automatically did as
she said, stifling a complaint about bossy women.

Sylvia glanced up to check the flow of fluid and frowned.
"Can you squeeze that bag? Make it run faster?"

"Yeah." He did as he'd seen the nurses in the ED, roll up
the empty end of the bag and put pressure on the fluid inside. He knew at the hospital they had a pressure sleeve for
that purpose. "Tell me what happened."

She touched the young man's neck, feeling for the pulse
there, and spoke distractedly. "We were packing them up to
go home—Alejandro, here, Danniqwa, and their baby. A car
drove past and someone shot him."

"His full name?"

"Alejandro Perez." She looked up at him and spoke carefully, deliberately. "He's a graduate student, a classical gui-
tarist. He was here for the birth of his first child, with the
woman who's been his partner for seven years, Danniqwa
Taylor. This is her first baby, too. She's a dancer—modern
dance. You might have heard of her troupe—"

She'd have gone on, but he interrupted, a bit harshly. *"I
get it.* Nice couple. Not a gang thug and one of his bitches."
He took a breath, notching down his anger. He hoped it
would work for both of them. "So that baby was just born?"

"Yes."

"I mean, here? Just now, tonight?"

"Yes. This is a birth center, it's what we do."

Good, he thought. She was trying. Her voice was calm,
despite the tone of forced tolerance. Clearly she'd had this
conversation before.

"Shouldn't she be in the hospital?"

"Who, Nicci? She's strong, healthy. She had a great,
normal birth. She's fine. So is the baby."

Cooper lifted his brow, skeptical. He thought about what

the young mother had just gone through and figured he'd want doctors, hospitals, and drugs, lots of drugs. That was the way his sister had given birth, with makeup and hairstyle carefully intact.

He shrugged and was glad to hear the sound of sirens. A moment later, the city ambulance and a squad car pulled up together. The paramedics greeted Sylvia by name. They listened to her concise report, accepting her assessment of the man's condition, then took over.

He watched that scene as he briefed the two cops. They were a pair he'd worked with before—Jackson and a new guy named Lawrence—who needed little instruction. They made short work of stringing police line tape and then began knocking on neighboring doors. It was likely a fruitless effort, but standard. Once in a while, they got lucky.

Alejandro was on a stretcher and being loaded into the ambulance before Sylvia let go of his hand. Then she went to the whimpering young woman on the steps and put her arms around her. She held both her and the baby, rocking and murmuring.

She spoke to Marisel. "They're taking him to Memorial. Call the labor unit there and tell the chief we want to admit a postpartum mother and baby. Then maybe you could drive them there? Stay with them until they get settled?"

Marisel nodded. "You'll be okay here alone with Tameka?"

Sylvia glanced up at a second story window that was faintly lit. "Yeah. She's early yet—only three centimeters when I checked her about an hour ago. Let's call my mom, though, and ask her to come down and help out."

"I'll do it." Marisel went up the stairs.

The young woman Danniqwa lifted her face to Sylvia. "Do we have to go to the hospital?"

The midwife stroked her face, spoke softly to her. "You don't have to. But I don't want you to be at home alone, and I thought you'd feel better to be near Alejandro. If you're at the hospital, they'll watch the baby in the nursery, and you can be there when he comes out of surgery."

Cooper admired the young woman's strength when she nodded and spoke the question that had put fear and despair in her eyes. "Is he going to be okay?"

Sylvia pressed her lips to the woman's forehead. "I think so, Nicci. He's strong, and he'll fight. He wants to be with you and Aniya."

The young woman smiled wanly and rested her head on Sylvia's shoulder. Her hand patted the baby's bottom. He wondered at the infant's silence, but could only see that she was snuggled into her mother's breast, apparently perfectly content.

Sylvia turned to Cooper. She was beginning to look a bit pale. He figured her adrenaline rush was about to drop her on her ass.

She wavered a bit, but spoke strongly. "Any chance you could move the baby seat over to Marisel's car? It's that green Forrester across the street."

Emilio, whose gaze had stayed on the door where Marisel had disappeared, looked at Cooper. "I'm on it."

Soon Marisel was back and Emilio helped the group get settled in the station wagon. Cooper turned to Sylvia. Her gaze followed the car as the rain and dark engulfed it.

"They named the baby Aniya. It means, look up to God."

He was quiet for a moment, watching her. The urgent need to act that had driven her for the last half-hour was gone now. She looked about to collapse.

He bit down on the urge to comfort. His fingers itched to take her arms and snug her up against his chest. He reminded himself of his job. "Did you get a look at the car the shooter was in?"

Instead of answering, she bent over, leaning with her hands on her thighs, her head down.

Cooper took her arms and raised her back up. "Are you okay?"

Her only response was a soft moan as she swayed a bit on her feet. He steadied her and she looked up at him. Without taking her gaze from his, she slowly slid one hand under her jacket. When she brought it back out, she held it between them, palm up. Cooper looked down and saw it was covered with blood.

"Shit." He grabbed her wrist. "Is that yours?"

She didn't answer, didn't take her eyes from his face. Cooper brushed her jacket aside and saw her white tee shirt was soaked with blood, from her ribs all the way down her right side. The black stain, glimmering crimson in the limited light, seeped into the jeans she wore.

"Baby," he said, not stopping to think about how improper that was. He took her up into his arms and looked around. The ambulance was gone. He carried her to the squad car, cursing himself for failing to take the basic step of ascertaining the number of injured. Where had he left his head?

"Emilio!" He called his partner over. "She's been hit. Get Jackson over here to drive us in." He slid into the rear seat, keeping her held tight in his arms. Soon Jackson was in the driver's seat, cranking the engine. Emilio held the back door open for a moment, giving Cooper a look.

Cooper met it, but had no explanation to give. "Oh, yeah—I think there's another woman in labor up there. You'd better stay with her until someone else gets here."

Emilio paled.

"Don't worry. She's only three centimeters—she's got some time yet." Now there was a little green around the edges of pale. "Help's coming."

Emilio seemed frozen, so Cooper pulled the door shut himself. "Let's go."

Tires squealed as they pulled out. Acceleration pressed him back into the seat and brought Sylvia's weight harder against his chest. He brushed strands of wet hair away from her face, stroking. Her eyes opened and he kissed her forehead, then tucked her head against his shoulder.

"I couldn't see the color of the car. It was dark. They didn't have their lights on."

"Shh." He kept his lips on her forehead, wondering at but accepting the pounding of his heart.

"The gun came out of the back window. It was rolled down, but not all the way, like one of those cars where the back window only opens half-way."

He shushed her again, biting back the word that was in his head—sweetheart. He enforced it this time by putting his lips to hers. When he lifted his face to look at her, she was watching him.

"Investigator—"

"Cooper."

"Cooper. You kissed me."

"Yes." He wanted more. He wanted to loosen her hair and bury his hands in it. He wanted the taste of her, the feel of her. He wanted her safe.

He squeezed gently where his hand held her against him. "Hush, please. Rest."

"I was shot, wasn't I?"

He nodded, fighting icy fingers of fear that nearly stopped his breath. He stroked her face as he felt the wetness of her blood saturate the leg of his jeans. He hardly knew her, but he wasn't sure he would survive losing her.

He could barely hear when she echoed his thoughts.

"What a strange night."

CHAPTER TWO

Sylvia took careful inventory before she moved, before she even opened her eyes. She was in a bed—one with the head raised, with a single flat, unobliging pillow. She heard the beeping of monitors, the persistence of alarms, tinny overhead pages for respiratory therapy and the code team. When she took a breath—a shallow, careful one—she caught the odor and knew where she was for sure.

She hated hospitals. Okay, so she'd worked in them from time to time. That didn't mean she wanted to *be* in one.

Everything about her hurt. Her right side, just below her lower ribs, was absolutely on fire. Compared to that, the rest was merely a dull ache—head, back, arms. Certainly taking a deep breath was a bad mistake—nothing dull about that frisson of searing pain.

Her mouth was dry as cotton. She tried to lick her lips but failed. The energy required was too great. A quiet movement stirred the air at her left, then a straw pressed against her lips. Instinctively she took a short sip, wanting more but not having the energy for it. The straw remained there, though, nudging.

"Take some more, honey. It will do you good."

Hearing that deep, rich voice was a comfort. Sylvia wanted to slip away into it.

"No, Sylvie. Come back. Open your eyes."

She did, hoping the woman appreciated the effort. "Venda? You always were a nag."

The large, ebony-skinned woman let out a throaty chuckle, one that had always given Sylvia pleasure.

"What are you doing here?" Sylvia was not entirely sure where "here" was, but she knew it was not the labor unit. Venda had been a patient care tech on the labor unit of Memorial Hospital for something like thirty years. Sylvia had known her for the last several of those years, first when she was a new nurse, thrilled to land a coveted labor and delivery job. Later when she'd become a midwife, before she left the hospital to build her birth center.

They still talked each month or so—Sylvia had every intention of eventually enticing Venda away from Memorial to work with her at Tynie's Place.

Venda spoke matter-of-factly. "You know we take care of our own. You're in the SICU, but you've been in our hands, too. Molly was your scrub tech. Wojo is your nurse."

Sylvia smiled at the mention of two of her favorite labor unit staff. Tess Wojokowski would take it personally if anything went wrong. She was in the best of hands.

"Just what were you doing, getting yourself shot like that?"

Sylvia's recollection of the night's events beckoned, then flooded into her mind. "Hmm. We'd just had a birth, a beautiful one. She was so strong. They're a great couple. They were ready to go home. We took them outside. Their car was ready for them, right at the curb." She had to swallow against the sorrow. "There was a drive-by."

Venda sniffed, a sound signifying disdain and a little sympathy. She was married to a city bus driver; the two of them worked hard in their jobs. They struggled, so far successfully, to keep their own boys off the streets. She had no respect for any mother who didn't do the same.

Sylvia closed her eyes, suddenly fighting tears, winning only because her body couldn't spare the fluid. The straw touched her lips again. This time she drank deeply.

"Alejandro Perez was the father. Do you know how he's doing?"

"He's still in the OR. They've used ten units of blood so far. Guess we'd all better go donate. You've gotten four yourself."

Sylvia turned her head, looked up to where her IV drip hung, and saw a unit of blood now nearly empty. Her stomach rolled and she fought a shiver.

Venda squeezed her hand, away from the IV site. "You're gonna be fine. We got you all patched up."

That took Sylvia's attention back to the fire in her side. "Did they cut me?"

Venda shook her head. "No. Peterson was your surgeon, and you know he's the best. He got the bullet out by 'scope. The blood loss was from the liver, but they were able to control the bleeding without removing any of it. You'll be good as new soon, only a couple small scars to show for it."

Sylvia blinked hard and squeezed back at Venda's large, warm hand. She closed her eyes against the sight of someone else's blood dripping into her, against the thought of scalpels and instruments breaching her skin, probing inside her.

She lifted her free hand to press against her mouth. There was a soft jangling sound and warm, smooth metal brushed her lips.

She opened her eyes and saw that a silver chain was threaded through her fingers, a cross dangling in her palm.

"Your man left that for you. He wanted you to know he'd be back as soon as he finished up his work." She paused and gave Sylvia a stern look. "You've been holding out on me." One of the woman's fondest wishes, expressed with harping regularity, was for Sylvia to have a good man in her life. And a few babies for Venda to help spoil.

Sylvia rubbed her thumb over the simple cross. She struggled for the last, hazy memories. Strong arms holding her close. Lips softly touching.

She looked at Venda. "His name is...Cooper. Cooper Billings. I don't really..." Know him, was what she'd meant to say. But the words wouldn't come. She made a point of being honest with herself. Somehow, she did know him.

Venda face was speculative then broke into a wicked grin. "I heard he was fierce when he brought you in, shouting orders even at Dr. Peterson. I'd like to have been there to see that."

Sylvia knew there was humor in that, but couldn't seem to focus enough to find it. She was straining for the memory: warm hands slipping the cross into her palm, weaving the chain around her fingers. Lips pressing hard once against hers, then whispering urgently into her ear. *Be strong, Sylvie. Stay with me.*

Exhaustion overcame her. Venda rested her hand down on the bed and gave her a pat. "You sleep now. Maybe he'll be here when you wake up."

Apparently saying it made it so. When she woke next the cross and chain were gone from her fingers. Instead, her hand was clasped securely in Cooper's. He sat on an institutional gray metal chair pulled up next to her bed. His head rested next to their entwined hands, sunk so deep into the mattress that little more than his burnished, tousled curls showed. Silver glimmered at his neck. He was asleep.

Sylvia's fingers tightened in a reflexive longing to tangle themselves in those curls. The movement caused him to stir. He lifted his head, eyes suddenly alert and seeking hers. His gaze scanned her intently for several moments, then, seeming satisfied, he smiled. He took her hand to his lips and began kissing her fingers.

"How are you feeling?"

Bewildered, she thought. Unsettled by the way it felt so right that he should be here, smiling and sweetly—extremely sweetly—kissing her hand. She answered hesitantly. "I'm okay."

He stood but leaned over her so his face was close to hers. With his free hand, he cupped her cheek. "You gave me a scare. You lost a lot of blood before I even knew you were hurt."

"I—I don't think I realized it myself. I didn't feel anything until they'd taken Alejandro away."

He nodded, his gaze on her lips.

Her mouth felt drier than it had before. "I'm not sure I know why you're here."

His eyes met hers and held. He stroked his thumb over her cheek. "I think you do. I hope you do."

Sylvia's breath seemed to catch, and she was mortified when he looked up to the monitor above her head. There, she knew, he would find evidence of the sudden spike in her heart rate.

He watched the blips for a few moments, then moved his gaze back to her. He held her hand to his mouth again, this time her left hand. His lips skimmed along her ring finger. "You're not married. Are you involved with someone?"

A shiver skittered down Sylvia's spine. She took a moment to wonder at it, as she'd not thought her body had the energy to spare for non-vital activities. But then, she must be recovering faster than she thought, because there was also a warm surge low in her belly in response to that thing he was doing with her finger.

Eyes caught in his, she shook her head.

"Good." It was said with certain force, implying more.

Like, *Then I won't have to kill anybody.*

"I will never in my life fall in love with a cop." Though it was true, it seemed ridiculously presumptuous to say. The whole situation was presumptuous, as they had only just met. Not even that, really. But Sylvia was sure she was interpreting his intentions correctly.

He did not seem offended by her words. There was a feral satisfaction, in fact, in the smile he gave her. And approval as he nodded his head, apparently pleased that she didn't pretend to misunderstand him. "We'll see."

With that entirely confident, annoying statement, he rested her hand down on the bed. Then he rubbed his thumbs over her forehead. "Go to sleep. Rest."

The warmth of his touch sank into her, and she felt the heaviness of her eyelids. She almost called him on his highhandedness, but his touch was so very soothing. She began to sink into sleep.

She heard the scrape of the chair and felt the mattress shift when he rested his head beside her again. Without opening her eyes, she lifted her hand and placed it on his head. The curls felt softer than they should. She twined her fingers into them and drifted. She caught herself at her last wakeful moment and gave the strands a tug. "What are you doing? Go home. You've been up all night, haven't you? You need to sleep."

He seemed unimpressed so she tugged again.

"Hey, I *am* sleeping."

"Not here. You need to lie down. Really sleep."

When she yanked again a bit harder, he grabbed her hand and held it in his. "I never pegged you for a shrew."

She bit back a smile, but she would have pulled his hair again given the chance. "Cooper. Go home."

"I'm not leaving you."

"I'm okay."

Silence.

"You can't sleep sitting there in that chair."

"I've done worse."

"No doubt. But not on my behalf."

"Neither of us is going to get any sleep if you keep harping like this."

Sylvia sighed, but knew when she was beaten. Using an unfortunate amount of effort, she inched her body over to the edge of the bed away from him. "All right. Lie down up here, then."

"No way. Stop moving like that. You're going to hurt yourself, or disconnect something."

"Come on. Lie down next to me."

"Not a chance. I've seen Venda. She outweighs me by forty pounds."

"Coward. Have it your way then. But I'm not going to sleep until you leave."

"You're wiped. I can easily outlast you."

"Hah. I'm a midwife. Don't you know babies all want to come at night? I have resisting the urge to sleep down to an art."

He raised his head and gave her a look. She opened her eyes wide, as though toothpicks propped them open. He clenched his jaw, and she knew he was biting down on a laugh.

Mumbling about a shrew and stubborn, too, he pushed the chair away. Gingerly, he lay himself down alongside her, staying to the extreme edge of the bed, not touching her in any way. "If I die at Venda's hands, it will be on you."

She would have smiled. She did, in fact, when she felt his hand snake gently across her abdomen, find a place without tubes or bandages, and take firm hold at her waist. Then she was gone into sleep.

It was not Venda who found them there together, though Cooper would have preferred it. He opened his eyes and knew in an instant the woman who stood at the bedside with the disapproving frown could only be one person.

"Can't say I've ever surprised my daughter in bed with a man before."

He took a moment to curse silently, but truth be told, he was glad to hear that was the case. Still, this was an awkward moment.

Sylvia's mother. Cooper figured Tameka must have popped a baby out faster than expected. Stifling a groan, he lifted his head and gave Sylvia a once over. She was sleeping soundly—no doubt aided by the morphine that ran through an IV pump. But her color was better; she looked restful, not sick.

"Uh—" With care, Cooper lifted up from the bed. When he was standing, he reached over and tried to look innocent until the woman across from him relented and shook his hand.

"I'm Cooper Billings, investigator with RPD. I was first on the scene. I brought Sylvia in."

The woman nodded. Her hair was the same golden brown as Sylvia's, but shot through with strands of silver. The blue eyes had the same softness, but also suggested a keen and, in this circumstance, at least, suspicious mind.

"Katherine Huston." She nodded toward the bed. "You seem to have an unusual devotion to your work."

In his head, Cooper cursed again as he felt his cheeks redden. Not many people could make him blush. "I didn't want to leave her. I was comfortable dozing in the chair..."

He motioned to the chair behind him, feeling for all the world like a guilty schoolboy trying to substantiate his story of innocence. "She insisted."

The blasted woman raised her eyebrows in a skeptical way, entirely too reminiscent of Mrs. Butterfield, Cooper's all-knowing, all-seeing fourth-grade teacher. Like Mrs. Butterfield, she knew the power of silence. So far, apparently, the explanation was unsatisfactory.

"I—I have intentions towards your daughter. Uh, honorable ones." God curse the woman, he sounded like an idiot. There was nothing for it, however, and damned if it didn't seem to be true.

Her eyebrow raised in a different way, not surprised so much as maybe a little impressed. "Does she know about this?"

"I think she's getting the drift."

"Um-hmm. Did she tell you she'd never fall in love with a man on the job?"

"Yes."

"And that hasn't deterred you?"

"Not so far."

The woman almost cracked a smile, he was sure. She nodded. "You just might do."

Cooper gave her a nod back, acknowledging his appreciation of her approval, however underwhelming.

"So—Venda says she's doing well?"

"Yeah. She lost a lot of blood. It was my fault. I didn't know she'd been hurt until the ambulance was already gone." Cooper took Sylvia's hand in one of his, rubbing his thumb over the now fragile-seeming bones. He remembered the strength he'd seen in her hands last night, knowing both hope and despair. He scrubbed his other hand over his face, considering how he was going to learn to live with the sense of failure that weighed on him now.

Katherine Huston reached out, encompassing both his hand and her daughter's in hers. He felt understanding and absolution in the touch, and had to struggle to steady his breathing.

It took a moment. Then he looked up at her, aware through that touch that the resemblance between mother and daughter was substantially more than just physical. "How about Tameka? She do okay?"

Katherine smiled. "She did very well—she had a little girl. Your partner did well, too, though I believe he would rather face a roomful of hardened criminals than another woman in labor. Tameka was a bit of a screamer."

Cooper huffed out a laugh, knowing he'd be able to give Emilio a hard time about that for the next month, easy. *Okay.*

He turned his hand over, gave the older woman's a squeeze. "I've gotta get cleaned up and check in downtown."

"I'll stay with her now. Thank you for bringing her here, for staying with her." Katherine looked up at him, eyes glinting a bit. "I expect I'll see you again."

Cooper smiled at her, then leaned over Sylvia. He touched his lips to hers before he walked away. "Count on it."

CHAPTER THREE

Cooper tried to convince himself that a shower, clean clothes—his bloodstained jeans were still on the bathroom floor, to be dealt with later—and three cups of coffee could make him feel ready to face a new day. He had to try harder as he walked through the squad room. Silence fell and curious eyes followed him. He knew it wasn't just his imagination.

By now, the story of where and how he had spent several hours of the night was sure to be well circulated. One would think the police force consisted of a bunch of old hens. No one loved gossip more than cops.

So he did the only thing he could. He put a scowl on his face, glared at a few men whose smirks were overly obvious, and barged through the room without stopping. He made his way to the corner where Emilio and he shared cubicles, the dividers between them removed more than a year before.

"Coop." Emilio leaned back in his creaky old chair.

Cooper knew he was not going to be able to bluff his way past his partner—Emilio could scowl way better than he could. He slumped behind his own desk.

"You done playing nurse-maid so we can do our work?"

Cooper gave him a direct look and reported formally. "Alejandro Perez came out of surgery in pretty bad shape a couple hours ago. The docs say it will be several more hours before we can get anything out of him—if ever. The second victim, Sylvia Huston, is stable. She got a look at the car, but probably not enough to be of much help. We can try running the auto make/model program by her—I think she'll be up to it when she wakes up. If she's not ready, we'll have a hard time getting to her. She's got a lot of friends at Memorial. Some of them are big."

He paused to measure his partner's response, but saw no signs of softening. Sighing inwardly, he continued. "As you have no doubt already detected, Perez was hit as he was leaving Tynie's Place. That's a birth center, apparently owned and run by Ms. Huston. His baby girl had just been born. He'd been there for several hours with his woman in labor; a lot of people might have known he was there.

"His girlfriend, Danniqwa Taylor, was sleeping when I left the hospital. Given that she'd spent the day in labor I didn't wake her." He waited for an objection to that, and continued when his partner remained silent. "We should be able to interview her today. I did speak with her nurse. Danniqwa told her that the Taylor family holds a grudge against Alejandro. The nurse thinks Danniqwa is afraid that members of her family may have been involved in the shooting." He looked mildly at Emilio. "What have you got?"

Emilio grunted and held the scowl long enough to let Cooper know he was not in a forgiving mood. "Ms. Huston does indeed own Tynie's Place. It's named for a baby girl Ms. Huston delivered when she still worked at Memorial. Tynie died of neglect at five days of age. Her fifteen-year-old mother left her alone in a ninety-degree apartment while she went out with friends.

"Apparently that pissed off Ms. Huston. She decided that taking good care of women and babies in a big medical center like Memorial wasn't doing enough to keep them safe. So she built a birth center in the 'hood."

Cooper raised his eyebrow and nodded, impressed. Emilio's voice had lost its edge—he was impressed, too.

"This from the elder Ms. Huston?"

Emilio nodded. "Katherine. She's a hell of a woman, too. She's a nurse, though not a midwife, I guess, as Sylvia is."

"You learn anything about what the hell a midwife is?"

"Uh-huh, I got quite a lecture. It's what you think it is. They deliver babies. In fact, they've delivered babies throughout all of human history. Obstetricians only got invented, I'm paraphrasing here, a few centuries ago, and they haven't always done a bang-up job of respectfully caring for women. That last may be a bit editorial—my informant could be considered a biased party. She's very proud of her daughter."

"Yeah. Protective, too," Cooper said. He rolled a shoulder, remembering with a little discomfort his meeting with Katherine.

"There's a rumor Katherine found you in Sylvia's hospital bed. Of course, I leapt to the defense of my partner, who is known for his cool-headed, controlled, professional behavior."

Cooper sank his face into his hands, elbows propped on the desk. "I don't know what happened, Emilio. I couldn't leave her."

"She's part of an investigation, man."

Cooper raised his head at the sharpness in his partner's voice. He deserved some, but not all of it. "She was a by-stander, a *victim*."

"Yeah. And a witness. What the hell are you thinking?"

"I think I'm in love." That, regrettably, came out in a pa-thetic moan.

Emilio snorted. "She's spent most of the hours since you met her in surgery. You fell in love with her while she was unconscious?"

"Christ. I can't explain it, Emilio. I don't know what hap-pened. I can't believe it myself. But I think it's real." Cooper surged to his feet, dragged his hands through his hair.

Emilio searched his face for a long moment. He found something that caused him to relent.

As he sank back into his chair, Cooper hoped it wasn't pity.

"Are you going to be able to work this case?"

Cooper gave him a level look. "Yes."

"We could have the lieutenant reassign it."

"This is our case. We're not giving it up."

"You'll think with your head? Not your—?"

Cooper slammed his hands on his desk and started to his feet again.

Emilio lifted his hands in innocence. "Heart. I was going to say heart."

Cooper bit down on his temper. He and Emilio had been through a lot together; the man had a right to ask. He nod-ded. "I can think with my head."

"Then let's get going, pretty boy."

Cooper groaned. He'd heard the phrase, "Let's get going, pretty boy," every morning for the first few months he worked with Emilio. It was meant to communicate to Cooper that Emilio had no expectation that his new partner—too young, too many college degrees, too much family money—would ever make a good, smart cop. Cooper hadn't heard the phrase for nearly two years now.

They figured on giving their hospitalized victims and witnesses the morning to rest and recover. Thus, they'd rousted Ricky Hernandez at the, for him, ungodly hour of ten o'clock. They suffered through the highly unattractive process of a drunk forced prematurely to consciousness, and now had him propped in a corner booth in his dingy local hangout. Ricky was forty but looked seventy. He was scarred and skinny, aged by a life lived dangerously—drugs, drink, and gangs. His hands shook as he gripped his shot of tequila. His bloodshot eyes were vague as he tested his memory.

"The Perez family been members of the Kings at least two generations."

The Latin Kings were one of two gangs in Rochester that could claim any real organization. Their roots were old and deep in Hispanic neighborhoods situated in the northeast corner of the city. Ricky was never a leader, but he'd been part of the Kings for two decades. Now he was grizzled and gray, no use to the gang. He passed his days in a haze of alcohol and marijuana, reminiscing with other retired Kings or, barring that, with cops willing to spot him a drink.

"Manny—he's dead now. He was a player in the organization. He had two or three sons after him. Manny's brother, too—I forget his name now."

"How about Alejandro Perez? He's twenty-four, tall, thin guy. Smart. Does he have ties?" Emilio's voice was low, heavily accented now.

Ricky took the shot glass to his lips and sipped sloppily. "Alejandro." He shook his head. "Manny's boys are Pedro, Ramon, and another..." A shrug. "The brother, I don't know. I know there are Perez cousins, but I don't got their names."

"He plays guitar."

A small light glimmered in the dull eyes. "Ah—the musician. The Perez boy that went to university. I did hear about him. He belonged to the brother." He swiped at his mouth with a dirty sleeve. "I hear he don't come home, acts like he's not family. He's not in the gang."

"Does that piss the boys off?"

Another shrug.

"Ricky," Cooper pressed, "would they want to hurt him for it? Take him out?"

That was clearly an affront, and the man bristled. "Nah. He's family, whether he wants it or not."

"How about the Rocks? Do they have anything against him?"

The Plymouth Rocks, named for their Plymouth Avenue neighborhood, were the second of Rochester's organized gangs. Naturally, the Rocks and the Kings had a serious and deadly rivalry.

"You never know about the Rocks."

There was a television news van at the entrance to Memorial when they pulled into the hospital parking lot. As they skirted the crowd in the lobby, Cooper put a hand on Emilio's shoulder and brought him to a stop. "It's the skank."

Emilio smiled and scanned the crowd. "You mean, the Honorable Mr. Parsons?"

Noah Parsons was a second-term city councilman with an eye on the mayor's job. A handsome, charismatic African American, he'd been raised solidly upper-middle class in a Webster neighborhood just off the lake. His father was a Xerox engineer, his mother an operations officer there. He'd gone to a private high school and Ivy League college.

Cooper and he had met at University of Maryland Law. He was always well prepped, though if he took part in any study group, Cooper never knew about it. In class, he wore tailored silk suits and schooled his rich, deep voice in cultured tones. At night, he liked flash. He drove a Mercedes CLK, drank Absolut in Baltimore's hottest nightclubs, and always had at least one extremely good-looking woman on his arm. He did not socialize with his classmates.

Back in Rochester, Parsons changed his appearance if not his character. He bought a house in the city and joined a local law firm that did a lot of big claim worker injury and medical malpractice. He found a wife, a tall, striking woman who quit her job as a patent lawyer to bear and raise his children.

After four years, he ran for city council. He wore his hair in braids and traded his suits for African print shirts and leather jackets. He added a touch of street to his language. His speeches were fiery, skillful oratory.

His predominant issue was the destruction of the city's neighborhoods caused by drugs and violence. He developed grass roots town meetings to address the fears and concerns of citizens. He slammed the police, alternating between complaints that they failed to secure the safety of the public and accusations of civil rights abuse when arrests were made.

Cooper admired the man's rhetoric, sometimes even agreed with it. He understood enough about politics to accept impersonally that the force made an easy target when votes counted more than honest discussion of the city's problems.

But everyone on the job knew most of the dirty little secrets in town. And one of Rochester's dirty little secrets was that Noah Parsons still liked nightclubs, still liked to have beautiful women on his arm. Even while his elegant wife was home with the kids.

The man was a skank. Cooper had suspected it before, in Baltimore. He knew it for sure now. Parsons knew he knew it, too, ever since they'd bumped into each other outside a club at two in the morning, while Parsons was helping one of his lovelies into a limo. When their eyes met, Parsons smiled, taunting. He put his hand on the woman's ass, giving it a carnal squeeze as she bent to get in. The message was clear: while Cooper finished out his night shift on the street, the councilman would be enjoying hot, illicit, backseat sex. Clearly, in his mind, he was the victor in his little one-sided pissing contest.

Since that encounter, Parsons had taken every opportunity to subtly harass Cooper. He called out as the camera crew packed up.

"Investigator Billings! Perhaps you'd like to comment on last night's shootings."

The news reporter looked to him, mike still in her hand. He nodded to her and she smiled. They'd dated a couple times, enough for him to know that her ditzy blonde looks that played well on camera covered a sharp, remarkably cynical mind. He turned his attention to Parsons. "Hello, Councilman. I'm sure Ms. Nasso is aware that comments from the department come through headquarters."

Jacquie made a show of turning off her mike and spooling up the cord, but she hovered close enough to easily listen in.

"I understand you spent the night in the hospital, Billings. Yet there were no reports of any police injuries." Parsons's smirk was just audible.

Cooper could feel Jacquie's interest. "I appreciate your concern, Councilman. I wasn't hurt."

"But you did spend the night here."

Cooper knew better than to rise to Parsons's bait, but his

partner's hand on his shoulder didn't hurt any.

Emilio broke in. "Investigator Billings brought in the injured woman, then came back to the precinct to file his report. When that was done, he returned to the hospital to check on the status of the victims and to interview if possible." He held the politician's skeptical gaze steadily. "Just as we are continuing to do now."

It was obvious Parsons longed to say more. Cooper could see him weigh the risks of speaking in front of a reporter when he had his own secrets to protect. Cooper lifted his brow, making a dare, and saw Parsons back down.

"Commendable effort, I'm sure. It's unfortunate that your ability to protect the citizens of Rochester is so limited. As this case demonstrates, not even our mamas and babies are safe."

Cooper rolled his eyes, visualizing Parsons kissing little Aniya Taylor Perez as the lead story on the evening news. He felt the hand on his shoulder press a little harder, turning him away from the confrontation.

Emilio nodded to Jacquie, then Parsons. "As we said, you can seek comments from downtown. Councilman, if you wish to review RPD's strategies for countering street violence, I'm sure Chief Laruso would be happy to meet with you. Now, if you'll excuse us, we have work."

They checked with hospital security and learned that Alejandro Perez was in guarded condition. He was in surgical ICU and had not regained consciousness. There was some swelling in the brain that might indicate neurological injury, a result of decreased oxygen from severe blood loss. Apparently the medical treatment for that was "wait and see."

Next, they tried Danniqwa Taylor. She was in her bed on the birth unit, resting with her baby asleep on her chest. When they quietly knocked, she opened her eyes and nodded them in.

"Ms. Taylor, I'm Cooper Billings and this is my partner, Emilio Navarre, Rochester PD." They showed badges, but she didn't inspect them.

"I remember." She met Emilio's eyes. "You helped us last night. Thank you."

Emilio motioned to a chair and with her permission pulled it up closer to the bed before sitting. Cooper stayed back and tried to look unthreatening. Emilio was a lot better at it, and began by admiring the baby.

"She's a beautiful girl." She was, too. All dark curls, plump cheeks, and bow lips softly open now and drooling in slumber.

Danniqwa smiled and stroked the baby's back. "Thank you."

"We got a report on Alejandro. Have you seen him?"

"Yes. I was up there this morning. They didn't tell me very much."

"Not us, either. I think they just don't know yet." He let a moment pass. "I'll say a prayer for him."

The young woman looked at him again, considering, then said a quiet thanks.

"You know why we are here, Ms. Taylor."

She looked away, bit her lip, and slowly nodded.

"Do you know who might have wanted to hurt Alejandro?"

Silently, without making eye contact, she shook her head.

"Do you have a guess?"

She closed her eyes and laid her head back.

"Ms. Taylor, let me tell you what we know. We know that many members of the Perez family belong to a gang, the Latin Kings."

She opened her eyes and turned on Emilio, anger flashing. He met her gaze calmly and continued. "We know that Alejandro is not a part of the gang, that he doesn't see his family much, if at all."

She nodded, calming.

"We also know that a young man whose last name was Taylor was killed in a gang shooting last winter. That was your brother, wasn't it?" He watched her, but she'd turned her face away again. "At the time, a rival gang, the Plymouth Rocks, blamed the Kings for Taylor's death."

He paused for another moment, then leaned toward her. "Ms. Taylor, we'd like you to help us find out who tried to kill your baby's father. If you won't talk to us, we'll have to wonder if you're trying to protect someone."

The room was quiet. The baby stirred and Danniqwa nestled her closer.

Emilio spoke softly. "I noticed that you and Alejandro were

alone there at Tynie's Place. The other girl who had her baby there last night, Tameka, she had a lot of family. They filled the waiting room downstairs; they cheered when the baby was born." She was quiet as she rocked her baby, tears now spilling down her cheeks. "Nobody cheered for Aniya."

He waited while she dealt with the tears. "I respect what you and Alejandro are trying to do, Ms. Taylor. I see that you are trying to make a good life for your little daughter, away from the drugs and the gangs. I can see that makes you alone.

"I understand that you would not want to talk to the police, that you do not want to betray your family. But it looks like you have chosen Alejandro over your family. Since you have, you should try to help us find out who shot him."

Danniqwa's jaw clenched. Bitterness laced her voice. "He's already hurt. You can't help him now."

"And if he survives? Will he be safe then? Will you be able to tell your daughter you did everything you could to protect him?"

She glared at Emilio through tears. Cooper sympathized with her for the bind she was in; he was impressed when he saw her relent.

Her head on her pillow, eyes closed again, she spoke softly. "My grandmother raised me. She died of a stroke just a few months ago. My mother died of AIDS that she got from my father. He used needles. My father had boys by two other women before he got himself killed in a robbery at a mini-mart.

"Nobody took in my half-brothers. They bounced around in foster care, then found themselves a home with the Rocks. Dontae was the one who was killed last winter. Word was that one of Alejandro's cousins was involved in that shooting.

"They never bothered with Alejandro—he's always made it clear he had no part in gang life." She paused, looked over at Emilio before she continued. "This wasn't a gang shooting. This was personal."

Emilio raised his eyebrows. "Personal?"

"Alejandro made me pregnant. A Taylor male would feel honor bound to punish a Perez who did that. Even if the gang wouldn't sanction it."

Cooper saw how Emilio stilled, how his eyes sharpened. "What does that mean, that the gang wouldn't sanction it?"

Danniqwa appeared aware of the change, too. She took a couple quiet breaths before she spoke again. "For the last few months, the Rocks have been acting different. They have—rules."

Her hesitation underscored the strangeness of such a concept. Cooper exchanged a look with Emilio, considering the implications.

Danniqwa continued. "Grievances are supposed to be brought before the gang, like a council. The council makes a judgment, determines punishment. The gang boys aren't supposed to act on their own."

"You think this shooting was someone acting on his own?"

"I heard my other brother, Antwan, spoke to the council last week. He did not get permission for a hit on Alejandro."

"How do you know about this? From Antwan?"

"No. He and I don't speak to each other. I have a friend from school who's hooked up with a Rock. He's on the council. She told me. I thought it meant we were safe."

"Do you think it was Antwan who shot Alejandro?"

She sighed, weary and helpless. "I don't know, really."

"Who knew you were in labor? Who knew you were at Tynie's Place yesterday?"

Danniqwa turned her head away, didn't answer.

"Did you tell your friend?"

She squeezed her eyes closed. After a moment, she nodded.

Emilio was silent. Cooper knew his partner wanted to quit, to leave this young woman alone to grieve and heal. He also knew it wouldn't happen yet.

Quietly, Cooper took over questioning. He asked about the change in the Rocks organization. She appeared to know little about it, just rumors about the council and a new chain of command. Hints that the gang's leader no longer acted on his own.

She wouldn't reveal the name of her friend and, no, the friend would not agree to talk to the police. Cooper knew that relationships in the gang were often short-lived, so he asked Danniqwa to let him or Emilio know if things changed for her friend.

By the time they'd gotten what they could from her, Aniya was stirring, needing to be fed. They left the young mother totally focused on her little one.

Cooper knew she'd dismissed them from her mind. She, like many in the city, would have little confidence that the police could do anything to stop the violence that threatened so many neighborhoods.

Cooper hoped they would be able to prove her wrong. When he joined the RPD three years ago, he immediately partnered with Emilio. Months later, Emilio's nephew, Eric, died in gang gunfire. Since then, Emilio had been on a mission; he was determined to end the killing. That was the reason they'd been on their way to Tynie's Place the night before. The tip they'd gotten about a hit had been dead on. Their source was good; they wished they knew who he was.

Sylvia Huston had been transferred to a post-op floor. When they found her room, Cooper paused at the door. Gold October sunlight slinked through a large window—her friends must have been watching out for her again. She dozed quietly in the mellow light, a book fallen closed in her lap. His heart settled as he watched her.

Doubts had ridden him throughout the day. Though he'd defended his feelings to Emilio, he felt half crazy himself. He'd said he was in love with a woman he didn't know, he'd spoken of intentions. He'd never had much respect for love; he'd certainly never had any experience with it. His parents had formed essentially a business union, tying together two wealthy old Baltimore families in the most practical of ways. He and his sister had been dealt with practically, too.

His sister had done as she was supposed to do: she got a degree in art history, married advantageously, and settled down to raise two children and attend charity board meetings and garden club fund-raisers.

Cooper had tried to follow the path set for him as well. He graduated from an excellent law school and moved into a well-respected corporate firm. He dated the debutantes he met at his parents' country club, even became engaged to one. But when he could not face one more day at the law firm, when he chose to follow his heart into law enforcement, well, the fiancée found someone else. She traded him in for a

Emilio came into the room and nodded. "Ms. Huston. I hope you're feeling better—you looked a little peaky last night."

"I'm feeling fine, Investigator. My mother tells me you make an excellent birth assistant."

Cooper thoroughly enjoyed the blush on his partner's cheeks, visibly enough to have Emilio scowling. "Yeah, well. That's not something I'd want to do every day. But the girl did fine, and had a pretty little baby, too."

"I heard you're going to be the godfather."

Cooper laughed out loud as the red of Emilio's cheeks paled to white. He heard him whisper, "*Santos mio,*" under his breath. Sylvia grinned, too, and he wasn't sure whether she was pulling Emilio's leg. If so, it was too good a joke to bust up.

He took Sylvia's hand again and nudged up next to her, resting one hip on the bed. She immediately scooted over to make room for him, then colored a bit herself as Emilio gave first her a look, then Cooper, then rolled his eyes. He hooked his foot into the leg of a chair and pulled it over to the other side of the bed. He signaled Cooper to start.

"We want to go over what happened last night, Sylvia. Alejandro is still unconscious, his condition a bit dicey. We spoke with Danniqwa. She and the baby are doing fine; they're supposed to go home tomorrow.

"She said that she and Alejandro had been at Tynie's Place since the morning, when her water broke." Cooper knew he hadn't kept the squeamishness out of his voice when Sylvia gave him one of those superior woman looks. Chagrined, he continued. "She said they were there alone, that they hadn't had any friends or family with them."

Serious now, Sylvia nodded. "That's true. They're estranged from their families. They're both very talented, and determined to make something of themselves. That makes them different from almost everyone they grew up with. Then they fell in love with each other—across racial and ethnic lines, and contrary to gang allegiances. That makes everyone they grew up with hate them."

Emilio spoke next. "Yesterday, while Danniqwa was in labor, were there any problems? Angry phone calls? Any fights or disagreements?"

Sylvia shook her head. "Nicci and Alejandro pretty much

"Tell us everything you can remember about the car."

"There were four doors, with the back window on the passenger side partway down. I already told that to Cooper, last night. There was chrome along the back edge of the window. The car was dark, but not black—maybe blue or a dark red."

"There was a street light at the corner, and another near you where the shooting took place. What color was the car when you saw it there?"

Sylvia paused, keeping her eyes closed, doing her best, Cooper knew, to work with Emilio. "Red—maroon."

Emilio spent an hour with her, until they were all sure she had remembered as much as was possible. With a laptop they reviewed the make/model automobile program in an effort to narrow down the car. They got close.

Sylvia responded with a tired smile when Emilio praised her efforts. Then he nodded at Cooper, showing he was impressed. "Meet me at the car. Five minutes."

Cooper rubbed his thumbs gently over her face, closing her eyes. "You did good, baby." He pressed his lips to her forehead. "I want you to sleep now." He could not seem to help that his lips lingered.

Her fingers wrapped around his wrist, he felt her thumb stroke over his pulse point. "Cooper."

His lips wandered along her jaw. "Hmm?"

"You know I'm not going to fall in love with you."

He reached the corner of her lips with his, hovered there, just touching, not quite a kiss. Her breath hitched as she drew it in, then escaped with the tiniest trace of a moan.

Keeping his grin to himself, he stepped back. "Yeah. So you said. We'll see."

CHAPTER FOUR

It was past seven when Emilio and Cooper got back to the station. The squad room was emptier, quieter. But the light was still on in the lieutenant's office, causing them to exchange an uneasy look.

Justifiably so, as they were not halfway through the room before the door opened and Travis Sullivan's gray head poked through. With an imperial nod, he beckoned them into the office.

Sullivan sat back in the plush leather seat behind his desk. Cooper had a sinking feeling when the lieutenant's stare held him hard. It worsened as the silence lengthened and there was no invitation to have a seat. It was all he could do to return the look and not fidget.

"Explain your involvement with the female victim in the Rosedale shooting."

Emilio, the turncoat, took a step back and leaned against the door. Cooper was pretty sure he could feel the smirk.

"Yes, sir. A woman by the name of Sylvia Huston caught a stray bullet. At the scene she was giving first aid to the intended victim, unaware herself that she had been hurt. By the time her injury was discovered, the ambulance had come and gone. I took her by squad car into the E.D. I was concerned about her condition and returned to the hospital after Emilio and I completed our initial report. I spent the rest of the night at her bedside."

He stuttered when Sullivan's brow lifted. Lesser men had been done in by it. "This—this afternoon, having ascertained that Ms. Huston's condition had stabilized, Emilio and I returned to interview her. She was a cooperative witness."

He trailed off as the brow remained lifted. He stood at attention until the lieutenant spoke. "I am curious as to your definition of the word, *bedside*."

"Uh, yes, sir. To be exact, I did for a short time lie down

alongside the victim in her hospital bed."

"You did."

"She insisted, sir."

"She did. And you, naturally, felt compelled to comply."

Cooper drew a deep breath. "I understand my behavior was inappropriate."

"*Inappropriate?* You've made this department vulnerable to charges of sexual assault."

"It wasn't like that—"

"Then perhaps you'd explain?"

Cooper dragged his hands through his hair. He glanced back at Emilio but found no help there. "I've developed a personal interest in the witness, sir."

"Has she said anything to encourage you?"

Cooper paused to consider that. He indulged himself for a moment with the thought of whether an interesting, interested little moan constituted verbal encouragement. He gave it up, as the lieutenant would not buy it, and the damned woman had done nothing verbally but discourage him. "No, sir."

"In that case you'll stay away from her, Billings. As it is, you're one step away from a formal reprimand."

"Sir—"

"Stay away from her, Coop."

Cooper let that order roll through him, trying hard to accept it. Lieutenant Sullivan was a good man, had supported him in his difficult early days on the job. He considered him a friend, one who didn't wield the power of his position carelessly. Still, he found himself shaking his head. "I'm not sure I can, sir."

Sullivan leaned back in his chair, his gaze heavy on Cooper. "The mayor got a call from Councilman Parsons this afternoon. The mayor talked to the chief. The chief talked to me. They want your badge."

Cooper felt a pressure in his chest that threatened to take his breath. Not much would cost him more than giving up his badge. He struggled to steady himself, to look back at his lieutenant. He did better when Emilio moved up to stand shoulder to shoulder with him. "Do I have to give it to them?"

Sullivan slowly shook his head, his arms crossed over his chest. "Not yet."

"You—" Cooper thought about it, knew that Sullivan had

put himself on the line for him. He would do it for any of his men, but... "Thank you, sir."

The older man nodded, acknowledging more than had been spoken. Finally, he gestured Cooper and his partner toward the chairs that faced his desk. He waited until they were settled and then looked from one to the other. "Does Parsons have anything against either of you?"

Cooper lifted a hand. "I knew him in Baltimore—we were in law school together." He explained how Parsons had lived high, aloof from his classmates. Then he told of the night in Rochester when Cooper had caught him in the midst of a sexual rendezvous.

"So he lives fast, cheats on his wife, and doesn't care if you know."

"He *likes* it that I know."

Sullivan nodded as the three of them considered the situation. "If there's more, find it." He pointed them out the door. "And, Coop, watch your back."

"Hello?"

"It's Coop." He listened to the silence in the short pause, wishing he knew what to make of it. He'd waited until late morning to call—he'd wanted the phone to himself, and Emilio would not be moved out of his chair until he had to be in court.

"Hello, Cooper." Not much to be read into that, though she did not sound unfriendly.

"How are you feeling?"

"I'm good, really. I'm getting discharged today."

He remembered her paleness. "You sure that's not pushing it?"

"I'm fine. I'll rest better at home." Home. He didn't know where that was. RPD did have certain resources, however.

"Can I give you a ride?"

"Oh, no, thanks." Humor tinged her voice. "I'm afraid it will be a bit of a circus as it is. My mother's coming, and I've got cousins. Thanks, though."

"When can I see you, Sylvia?"

The humor was gone. "Coop—"

"Soon, Sylvie. It's going to be soon."

"We've got five maroon, four-door '96 Cutlasses registered in Monroe County. One is on East Ave. and three in the 'burbs. One is registered to Rashad Williams, lives on English Drive."

Cooper's eyes met Emilio's at that. Marisel was a good witness, too, and with her help they'd nailed the make and model. "Rashad's our guy. Shall we go say hello?"

Emilio shook his head. "What we really want is to bring in the car, get prints."

"Yeah, but we won't get a warrant. I mean, you and I know the driver doesn't live on East Ave or in Pittsford, but the judge will need more."

"We need to put Rashad in with the Rocks."

"Yup."

"We need Sunday."

Sunday was the name they'd given to the unknown source who was feeding them information on the local gangs. They'd first heard from him about two years earlier—he'd called on a Sunday morning, on Cooper's home line. Several Sundays he'd contacted them, giving them the who's who of the weekend activities. He called from pay phones and initially would only talk to Coop's answering machine.

After a few weeks Cooper waited for the call, and then they thought they'd lost him. When Cooper answered, the young man hung up. The next week, when the phone rang, Coop picked it up. Into the phone, he said, "This is Coop. Leave a message." He pressed a number to make a beep, and the kid went for it. Halfway through the "message," Coop slipped in a question. After an anxiety-provoking pause, the informant kept talking.

He never gave a name, would never agree to a meet. They had no way to reach him. But gradually he increased the frequency of his contacts. Cooper gave him his cell phone number, but the informant never used it. He did sometimes send text messages to Coop's pager; that was how they'd managed to nearly make the shooting in front of Tynie's Place.

Pay phones and electronic messages sent from Spot and other coffee/internet shops. They could not track the young man and they never tried too hard. He was good; his information was never wrong. They valued him enough to protect him, and accepting his anonymity was a good way to do that. Someday they might need to bring him in, but for now they could wait for Sunday.

That left Cooper with a quiet Saturday afternoon. He owned an old two-story in the South Wedge near Highland Park. The Olmsted-designed park was a jewel, filled with beauty year-round. Its trails were great for his daily runs and he cursed the hills only on bad days. When he needed flat, he headed for the Erie Canal towpath. But he loved the park and only stayed away from it during the week of the Lilac Festival. At the end of the annual event, he cleared his yard of the paper plates and cups left behind by the lilac fans and got his park back.

He loved his house, too. Built into the hillside, his wide front porch had a great view of downtown. From his upstairs bedroom, on clear days when the leaves were gone, he could see light shimmering off the lake. When there was light.

The house was solid, built of stone and wood and stucco. Inside there was lovely, deep walnut buried under layers of paint. Slowly he was removing the paint and polishing shine into the rich wood. He'd completed work on the first floor, all except for the kitchen. He didn't spend much time there; vaguely he thought to save that job for a woman's direction. Now he was tackling his bedroom.

He spent the morning sanding. It was satisfying work, but a job that left the mind free to wander. He sanded, then rubbed his thumb over smooth wood. Then he remembered rubbing his thumb over smooth skin, and his mind was gone.

He gave token resistance, but caved by early afternoon. He showered, dressed again in jeans and a soft cotton sweater, and went out back for flowers.

Sylvia was taking a restful day, despite the skepticism of friends and family who called regularly to check on her. She was settled on the couch in her living room, with blanket and pillow and a paperback. She even had a fire flickering nicely along in the fireplace, compliments of her cousin Jed who had dropped by with Aunt Marge's chicken soup and double fudge brownies.

She decided she felt better than she should expect. She

was not big on moving—nearly any activity brought pain. She felt chilled all the time and stayed wrapped in the blanket wherever she went. But all in all, for someone who had had a bullet taken out of her four days ago, she couldn't complain.

Except for the phone calls, which were frequent this morning, and the visitors arriving with food or flowers. Both dwindled by mid-afternoon, however. She hoped the word was out that she was behaving herself and didn't need any more reminders to take it easy. Because a nap sounded pretty good.

She dozed off, groaning awake when the doorbell rang. It felt like only two minutes later, but she saw that the fire had died to embers and knew she'd slept for a while.

She gathered herself for a moment, trying to figure out how to get up off the couch with the least pain. Once she was up, she toddled toward the door. Her hair was a mess and she probably had pillow lines on her face, but she didn't bother with any of it. One more cousin or auntie would have to accept her as she was. She just hoped she didn't have drool running down her chin, and swiped at it with her blanket in case.

Sylvia opened the door. Cooper stood on her front porch, tall and strong and handsome as sin. He wore a cream-colored sweater that hung loosely at his waist but snugged over the muscles of his arms and shoulders. Aged denim clung tightly in places that, once noticed, brought heat to her cheeks. Soft leather boots clad his feet. He stood like he was an oak planted there; he would not be moved easily.

Suddenly she wished she'd taken a little time to straighten herself. She revised that thought immediately, reminding herself that she didn't care what kind of picture she presented to this man she was not going to care about. She had to send that reminder to her heart, too, which seemed bent on racing along at twice its normal speed.

Slowly, aware of how vulnerable she felt, she took her gaze from his feet to his eyes. They were dark blue, the sky just before sunrise, and they'd been waiting for hers. They flashed with heat when her eyes met them.

Her breath, like her heart, quickened. His gaze was steady and held hers, like that oak, giving the feeling that he would be there forever. She resisted the urge to fall into it, to become lost in it. But that took a lot of effort, and so she stayed posed there, unable to move.

After a long moment, he reached out and opened the screen door. Without its meager protection, she felt defenseless, and those blue eyes took possession. At his unspoken direction, she stepped back.

He gave a single nod at her compliance and stepped through the door. He scanned her living room and seemed to settle in as though he found it comfortable. He obviously noticed the abundance of flowers, looking a bit chagrined as he held out his own bouquet. "I guess flowers were the wrong choice."

Finally she found her voice. "Thank you. Flowers are never wrong. Same goes for chocolate, by the way. Though I'd have to send you away if it had been more chicken soup." She took the flowers and breathed their scent—mums, late season roses, and rudbeckia, with some interesting dried grasses and red leaves. She looked up in surprise. "You picked these yourself."

A brow lifted and he toyed with a grin. "Yeah?"

"I mean, from where?"

"I sneaked over my neighbor's fence and raided her flower beds?"

"You have gardens."

"Do I?"

She liked the grin he let loose, a little dangerous though it was. She "humphed" at his reticence, and motioned him further into the room.

Before he moved, he put a hand on her arm, keeping her near as he looked her over. The heat of his hand warmed her through the blanket, more than the fire had, more than turning up the thermostat three times had.

He rubbed a thumb under her eye. "You look beat."

"I feel okay." His look revealed his skepticism—she was good at recognizing it now—it was the same look she'd seen in friends and family all morning. She lifted her chin in annoyance. "I do."

"Uh-huh. Go sit down." There really was not a choice about it as he had her in hand, leading her to the couch. He settled her in the middle with her feet up on the coffee table. Then he took the flowers from her and disappeared into the kitchen. When he returned, he went to the fireplace, added wood, and had a blaze roaring again.

He came back and perched next to her, hands touching, bringing that heat. "What can I get you? Juice? Tea?"

Hairbrush? she thought. *Toothpaste and a little lipstick?* His eyes were warm, compelling, and she was aware of how tempting it was to sink into his caretaking. He was the kind of man who would take responsibility for a woman, and take it seriously. There was danger in him for a woman who valued independence, who thought a woman should have her own strength. A very seductive danger.

She pulled herself back. "Orange juice would be good. There's some in the fridge."

He heard her hesitation. "And?"

She frowned, then gave it up. "Some ibuprofen. There's a bottle on the counter. Three, please."

He frowned back. "Ibuprofen? That's all you're taking?"

She nodded. "I'm fine with it."

He sent her a look but got up and went to the kitchen. When he came back he carried a big glass of orange juice. He crouched before her and opened his hand, revealing two of the prescription pain pills she'd been given.

She shook her head. "I don't want those. They make me feel terrible. I can't keep my eyes open."

"Closing your eyes is a good idea. Take them."

Stubbornly, she shook her head again.

Gently, he stroked his fingers over her face. "You're in pain. Please take them."

She had a sudden need to fight tears. To fight the urge to burrow into his chest, curl up, and wallow in the comfort he offered. She drew a deep breath to find herself. When he pressed the pills into her hand, she took them down with a swallow of juice.

"Good girl."

She huffed her objection to that. Then he sat next to her and before she knew it, he pulled her up onto his lap. She rested against his shoulder and the arm of the couch, still tucked in her blanket. "This is not a good idea. I'll fall asleep on you."

He ran fingers over her face, making her eyes fall shut. "Sleep is good."

What was good was the touch of his fingers. They soothed and calmed, took away pain and all thought. "I mean it. I'll fall asleep, and what will you do?"

She was not sure, but she thought lips had joined the fingers touching, stroking.

"No problem. I've got a remote. I've got football. I'm good."

He was good. His touch was magic. She was sliding into sleep, truly comfortable for the first time in four days. "Don't you need, like, beer and potato chips?"

"Next time. Sleep, baby."

His lips touched hers briefly. She sighed and let go. She felt him reach for the remote. He might have found a game to watch, but he left it muted so she could only guess. And that took too much effort, so she settled in, luxuriating in his touch.

She was almost gone when his lips whispered at her ear. "Sylvie?"

"Hmm?" Like a cat, she rubbed her cheek against his shoulder where his heat enticed.

"What do you have against cops?"

Something about the question almost brought her back, but she couldn't quite grasp a reason for it. "Hmm?"

He nudged at her, his forehead against hers. "Tell me. Why won't you fall in love with a cop?"

"Oh. They die."

"They die?"

"Um-hmm. They get married, have a little girl, and then get killed on her eighth birthday."

His strong arms hugged her to him and rocked her. She slept, safe.

Cooper held her as she slept for more than four hours. He sat through a couple good college games, but his thoughts were more on the woman in his arms.

So she was a cop's daughter. A dead cop. Somehow he was not surprised. She was strong, determined. The kind of daughter a cop would try to raise. A lot, he guessed, like her mother—the kind of woman a cop would try to marry. Strong enough to love a man on the job, to live with risk and uncertainty.

He thought about Katherine Huston. She'd survived her

husband's death without bitterness. At the least, she didn't seem to hold Cooper's chosen career against him.

The daughter was a different story. She'd never a choice about her father; she was born to him, and she loved him. But, obviously, she figured she did have a choice now. She figured she could choose whom to love, and she wouldn't choose a cop.

He held her in his arms, idly watched the games, and plotted. She was physically responsive to him, despite her intentions. She might have a strong will, but he had her weakness.

When she woke the sun was gone. Light flickered from the TV and the fireplace, but the room was in shadows. She was content, blissfully so, and nearly sank back into slumber.

Then she remembered in whose arms she'd fallen asleep. She opened her eyes, turned her head carefully.

She was still in his arms, though they were both curled up on the couch now. His back was against the sofa and she was snugged up against him, head resting on his shoulder. His arms were fast around her, even while he dozed. Or maybe he didn't doze, for as she moved his large hand squeezed gently at her waist.

His eyes were closed but lips touched her temple. "Feel better?"

She took inventory and was surprised. "I do. A lot."

The lips began a trail down her cheek, hovering near her mouth. "I told you sleep was good."

She let him have the smugness she heard in his voice, and smiled. She regretted that in an instant, though, as it brought the corner of her mouth into direct contact with his lips. He took immediate advantage, pressing his mouth firmly against hers. He moved a hand to her nape, precluding any thought she might have to pull back.

His lips were warm, heated. Coaxing, they rubbed against hers. He rose a bit above her, then leaned into her with a little of his weight. His breathing turned audibly wanting. With his hand along her jaw now, he commanded her to open for him.

Her own breath came out in a moan as she complied. His tongue touched hers, gently at first. Of its own accord her hand reached up to tangle fingers in the soft curls at his neck. He read the consent in that and sank deeply into her mouth. The heat of him suffused into her. She felt taken by him, owned.

That feeling increased as his hand left her jaw and stroked down her neck, kneading, rubbing. He followed the line of her shoulder until his hand grasped her upper arm and held firmly. He pulled her more tightly towards him, an action that dragged his forearm and wrist across her breast.

She could not hold back the little exclamation of pleasure brought about by that aching pressure. She was torn between the heat it stirred low in her belly and the fear it struck in her heart. Her fingers left his hair to grasp at his forearm; she knew before she tried that it would not be moved.

Fear won. She pressed her head back into the cushion beneath her, trying to get some distance from him. He let her go, and she knew it.

She had to try a second time to steady her breath when she opened her eyes to the sharp, piercing desire in his. "You keep kissing me."

His gaze fell to her lips; she could still taste him there. "Yes, I do. It turns out I like it. A lot."

"I told you about my father, didn't I? That wasn't a dream, was it?"

"You told me."

"Then you should understand."

"I do understand. But still, I'm going to kiss you." Intention, determination burned as his voice deepened. "And more."

"No." She closed her eyes, shaken by the thread of panic in her voice. He was quiet, waiting. "You shouldn't have your arm on my—my breast, either."

"Hmm. If you're complaining about that, you must not have noticed where my leg is."

She didn't dare open her eyes; the heat she felt in her cheeks would only get worse if she did. But she could feel him then, in a way she'd missed before he drew her attention to it. His leg was between hers, pressing up high into her center. And tucked against the soft nook where her leg joined her hip was his erection, long and very hard.

Maybe she had been aware. She had a little memory of arching up against him, seeking his hardness, seeking him. Mortified, she groaned, turning her head away.

He had the gall to laugh and give her a comradely pat on the hip. Then he swung up, bringing her up to sit next to him. "Come on."

"What now?"

"It's time to feed you. How about some of that chicken soup?"

She felt slow, her mind wading through mud, unable to keep up with him. She gave up, putting her elbows on her knees and dropping her head into her hands.

He put his arm around her shoulder and gave her a squeeze. "It's okay, baby. I'll take care of it."

"Do you know that 'baby' is really not the thing to call a grown, adult, responsible woman?"

"Whatever you say, sweetheart."

"Are you trying to be annoying?"

"A number of women have thought I didn't have to try."

"I have to wonder if I should be surprised at that."

"Probably because your brain is a little fuzzy from those pain pills."

She gave up, smiled, and leaned into him. "Chicken soup, huh?"

"Yeah."

"And brownies?"

"You bet." He smiled, too, then nudged her chin with a knuckle. "Would you like a soak in the tub while I get it set?"

"With you around? I don't think so."

His knuckles trailed away in a caress. "That's my girl. Uh, woman."

She admitted to herself she enjoyed the tease in his words.

"Sit tight. I'll be right back."

She minded his instructions only until he disappeared into the kitchen. Then she forced herself to her feet and tottered up the stairs to her bedroom. She went to her bathroom and moaned when she saw her reflection over the sink. She dragged a brush through her hair and then reached for the toothpaste.

CHAPTER FIVE

They'd not heard from Sunday, and so on Monday afternoon, after having spent the morning in court, Cooper and Emilio labored at their desks, grimly tackling paperwork. In the evening, Emilio planned to troll the gang neighborhoods, to see if he could come up with a line connecting their friend Rashad with the Plymouth Rocks.

Formally, the RPD did not acknowledge the presence of gangs in Rochester. For the public, for the press, police representatives referred only to loose alliances of young men participating in drug trade, robbery, and bullying that sometimes turned violent.

In truth, the local gang activity was nothing like the highly organized, and franchising, businesses that the Crips and the Bloods had developed in Los Angeles. But it was enough to keep neighborhoods of the city under siege, children closeted indoors, businesses failing.

Traditional strategies were successful only to a limited extent. Like when a street drug market became too open or threatening and police flooded the area. They'd round up and arrest everyone present. Some charges stuck and a few dealers would be off the street. But there were always others to take their place. And the large number of arrests led to complaints of harassment and strained relationships between the department and neighborhood and church groups that also worked to counter gang culture.

Working in Baltimore, Cooper had learned a more effective tactical plan. He saw the futility of Rochester's approach and had worked to develop support for change. Now, RPD was rolling out the new strategy.

He'd laid the groundwork for it soon after his transfer. Emilio, torn up by his nephew's death, began prowling the streets incessantly, cuffing and bringing in gang members for any observable offense. Cooper sympathized with the man's intentions and admired his tenacity, but he also saw the fruitlessness.

He chose a sunny Sunday morning in September. He rousted his partner out of bed—told him his date for the Bills game had stood him up—and forced him into a road trip to Buffalo. They sat out in the sun, drank a couple beers, and booed as the Bills got creamed. On the ride home, Cooper told Emilio about the strategy that Baltimore had used to fight street-level drug dealing and gang crimes.

Emilio may not have been ready to give his partner any credit for being a good cop, but he knew a good idea when he heard one. Together they researched the tactic. They took another road trip—this time to High Point, North Carolina, where the strategy had first been implemented, and to the Harvard professor who developed it. When they were ready, they went together to present it to Central Investigation Division.

CID was slow moving, but eventually it embraced the strategy. Cooper and Emilio headed the implementation task force.

The strategy coordinated efforts among neighborhood groups and churches, city police, state and federal prosecutors, and the probation and parole systems. It made use of intelligence-based "needle-strike" arrests rather than the haphazard "shotgun" approach traditionally applied. The task force targeted several neighborhoods that were particularly affected by gangs. The group spent nearly a year developing the crime "dossiers" of major players.

When they were ready for a particular neighborhood, they sent the message out to their targets. It was a "we've got you" notice. The targets were given a choice: clean up, get out of town, or spend a long time in a federal prison.

Supports were in place for those who chose to clean up. They were offered city jobs, drug-testing mandatory. Church groups organized food banks for families, acknowledging that drug trade was often a family's only source of income.

It was too soon to judge whether the tactic would have long-term success. They'd had positive press coverage and support from some community leaders. But there were always plenty of people happy to criticize any police effort.

The strategy had produced great intelligence contacts, in any case, and Emilio and Cooper used them to draw a bead

on Rashad Williams. Cooper finished a telephone conversation with Rashad's probation officer just as Jackson, the
young cop who had driven Cooper and Sylvia to the ED,
poked his head around the cubicle wall.

Jackson was a brawny, athletic type. He liked to wear
cowboy boots with his suits, which tended towards navy pol-
yester. He didn't make a show of it, so it could take a while
to figure out he had brains, if no fashion sense. He gave
Cooper a look-over, enough to have him raising his eyebrows
in question.

"I heard you used to play some ball. That you quarter-
backed." He continued when Coop nodded. "You any good?"

"I can throw."

"You play any recently?"

"I join the Saturday afternoon pick-up game at Cobb's
Hill once in a while."

Jackson nodded, assessing. "We have a traditional fall
game, the force against the firefighters. It's coming up in a
couple weeks." He might have seen some amusement in
Cooper's face. If he did, he objected to it. "It's serious ball,
man. We don't like to lose."

Cooper raised his hands, meaning no offense.

Jackson relented, continued. "We lost our QB. Tore up his
knee playing basketball yesterday. What do you say? Want
to join us?"

Cooper understood they were desperate, coming to him.
His pretty boy label had not been shed entirely. "Sure. I'd be
happy to."

"'Kay. Great. We practice Wednesday evenings, anyone
who can get the time off. And Saturday mornings. We usually use the East High field. I'll let you know."

Cooper nodded, then watched, curious, as Jackson hung
at the corner of his desk. "Yeah?"

"I, uh...I just wondered if you can take a hit."

He sat back, arms crossed over his chest. It wasn't the
usual question for a quarterback. As a matter of course, a
quarterback was given pretty good protection. "You got a
problem with your offensive line?"

Jackson looked offended, then reddened. "No, nothing
like that." He paused, waved away the concern. "It's just,
like I said, serious ball. Anyway, thanks. I'll be in touch about
Wednesday."

Jackson disappeared, and Cooper was left to ponder Emilio's grin. He wasn't explaining, either.

Cooper stopped by the birth center Thursday afternoon, around five-thirty. He thought he might catch Sylvie about closing time, talk her into dinner.

He'd left her late on Saturday night. After he fed her, pretty good chicken soup and darn good brownies, he talked a couple more pain pills down her. After that she was a goner. She probably didn't even remember him tucking her into bed. There were some lingering kisses, but she was so looped he couldn't in good conscience take advantage. He took himself home to a cold shower.

He hadn't contacted her since. He hoped he had her wondering, thinking about him. As strategy went, it was weak—he didn't really know if she'd given him a single thought. The truth was, a little distance felt necessary to him. When he had her in his arms, when she responded to his touch, well, nothing had ever felt more right. Or more powerful. It was enough to give any man a case of nerves.

He was entertaining forever kind of thoughts and doing so without breaking out in a sweat. It was unsettling, though. Something a man had to take some time with.

Enough was enough, however, and he'd spent the last couple days itching to be with her, to touch her. So he climbed off his bike—a sleek black Harley, plenty of chrome—outside Tynie's Place. He stifled a groan as he moved—aches and pains reminded him of practice the night before. He had a couple good receivers, a fine running back, and his protection had been more than reasonable. But Jackson had been right; even in scrimmage, these guys were serious.

Stretching to loosen muscles in his back, he limped up the steps. It was dusk now, but the sky was clear. Maples out front of the building were a nice golden orange and a very pretty mix of fall flowers lined window boxes and planters. He wouldn't admit to anyone that he could name them all.

The birth center was warm and inviting in a way he'd not appreciated the night of the shooting. There was also a surprising amount of activity. He opened the door hesitantly and walked into a hubbub.

The entrance was large with rooms off to either side, wide, polished wood stairs going up, and a hallway leading towards the back of the building. The walls were sunshine yellow with stenciled greenery making a garden effect. Live plants abounded. An aquarium bubbled, brightly colored fish darting around little castles and shipwrecks. On a table near the door sat a basket filled with condoms.

To the left of the entrance was a kind of living room—TV, lots of couches and big, comfortable-looking chairs. One wall was covered with tack board. On it were pictures—babies, families. Plenty of them featured Sylvie smiling and making eyes at a newborn. Also there were notes, thank-you's, dedications. And scattered everywhere, baby footprints with names and dates of births.

He guessed it was a family gathered in the room—African American, from young to old. A grandmother rocking a toddler, two young brothers or cousins watching *Reading Rainbow*, a couple girls giggling over a teen magazine. A young man on a cell phone.

To the right, beyond the stairs going up to the second floor, was a more formal-looking meeting room. In it, furniture was arranged in a large circle. Marisel was meeting with a group there—teen girls, some with babies or toddlers in their laps, some pregnant, some neither. They were a diverse group, a better mix of race and ethnicity than usually found comfortably gathered in one room. The discussion seemed to have to do with sex, and Cooper prudently tried to back away. He figured the family in the first room looked safer.

Marisel caught him, though, and beckoned him in. She walked to him with a hand extended and a friendly smile. "Investigator Billings."

He smiled back, but his heart wasn't entirely in it. He was very aware of the interest of the girls in the room. "Hello, Marisel. Call me Cooper."

When he took her hand, she pulled him further into the room. He couldn't figure out how to resist without looking like a coward, though it was tempting not to care.

"This is one of our groups. Girls, this is Investigator Billings, with the Rochester Police."

He liked to think the thing that kept them from rolling their eyes was his manly presentation, but he noticed Marisel was giving them a sharp eye.

"He was here to help the night that Alejandro Perez was shot. He took Sylvia to the hospital and stayed with her until

Mrs. Huston got there." That won some approval and the looks from at least some of the girls approached friendly.

Then Marisel smiled in a way he determined never to trust again. "Maybe one day the Investigator will join us in a meeting, give us a man's perspective." That had the crowd grinning lewdly, he thought, and Cooper sweating.

"Yeah, sure." *Not in this lifetime.* Some of the girls were smothering giggles, he was certain. "Uh, is Sylvia here?"

Marisel took pity on him, telling the girls to continue their discussion, then walking him back out of the room. "Sylvie's upstairs with a labor. I'll run up and see if she can step out for a minute. Come back this way."

She took him around the stairs to an office further back in the building. As in the living room the furniture was comfortable—chosen, he guessed, to be conducive to napping. He inspected the room when Marisel left him.

There was a library of textbooks and journals—midwifery, obstetrics, a smattering of other medical and social topics. A desk with several files on it was tucked in the same corner, near enough a window for a view. There was a small kitchen area: an under-counter refrigerator, a microwave, countertop and sink. A cinnamon scent lingered.

The long, deep couch had a reading lamp at one end, blanket and pillow tucked at the other. There were a lot of plants, taking over in some spots—an ivy was trying to creep around the bottled water stand—but appearing well loved.

There was pretty good art on the walls—local painters, Cooper noticed, some who were gaining national attention. And pictures—these of family. Sylvia as a young girl, fishing with a man he assumed was her father. Sylvia's mother with her arm draped around another woman, both of them smiling happily. He was getting interested in a couple photos of Sylvia with a man—big blond, friendly looking—too friendly to suit Cooper—when he heard her at the door.

He turned, the photograph forgotten as he drank her in. "You don't look that bad."

She raised a brow, communicating that she was unimpressed with his observation. But she seemed much better—energetic, healthy and strong again. He felt a deep relief and an equal surge of desire. Drawn, he moved toward her.

He moved close enough to touch. He slid his finger along a loose curl, brushed his thumb along her cheek. "I mean, you look healthy, recovered. It goes without saying that you look good."

She smiled, but he saw the indulgence in it. "I mean it. You took my breath away when I first saw you, and then you had a bullet in you. Even after you'd just come out of surgery, I wanted to—"

There was more amusement in her face as she waited for the end of that sentence.

"Well, you're beautiful."

She giggled and he pressed his lips against her laughing mouth. "Hello, Sylvie."

She pulled back before he could make anything of the kiss. "Hello, Cooper."

"You are feeling better, right?"

"Yes, I feel fine. Thank you." She sobered, and his heart thudded as she lifted her fingers to his cheek. "You took good care of me on Saturday."

He turned his face so his lips were on her fingers. He liked it a lot that she left them there long enough for him to nibble, to taste. "You didn't mind that I had my way with you after I drugged you senseless?"

"I did feel a little sore when I woke up on Sunday."

He shot her a look in panic. "Sylvie, I didn't—That was a joke—"

Then she laughed, spilling over with it when she caught the look on his face.

"You're a brat." He grabbed her up, kicking the door shut behind her before he moved to the sofa.

"What are you doing?"

"Well, I came here thinking I'd take you to dinner, you know, maybe get you in the sack later." She laughed again and he knew he had to make this woman his. "But I'm getting that you're busy here. So I figure the least I should get is a little necking on the couch."

He put her on the couch and followed her down, covering her, letting her have a lot of his weight. He kissed her and when she gasped for breath, he took her mouth. She responded sweetly, hotly, her hands clenching at the back of his shirt. Pulling him into her, God bless.

He pillaged her mouth, hardening against her. He rocked into that soft place at the juncture of her thighs, that place he knew was made just for him. When he finally had to come up for air, he held her face between his hands, staring down at her.

Her breath was unsteady. She sank her head into the cushion for a little distance, but kept her fingers tangled in his hair. "Necking? That's necking?"

He pressed a little into her, moved one of his hands lower, nearly to her breast. "Full contact necking."

She almost managed a laugh, but the breath caught and she arched just a little. Invitation or no, Cooper moved his hand until it covered her breast. He rubbed his palm over it and could feel the tight nub of her nipple. He pressed against it, harder. She let out a moan that turned into a little mewing sound.

"Coop."

"Sylvie." He took his mouth back to hers, still holding her gaze, letting go only at the last minute. He kissed her gently now, awed, grateful beyond words for her responsiveness to him. He drew his tongue along her cheek. "Sylvia, I have to have you."

"Cooper." She took a breath, sighed it out. "I'm working, I have someone in labor."

He laid his head along hers, watching her, willing himself to settle. "And so what? A quickie on the couch is, like, inappropriate? How do you think that baby got made?"

She huffed out a laugh. She moved his hand from her breast but didn't take it far, merely rested it over her abdomen, her own hand holding it there. She turned her face toward his and he saw something in it—pleasure, warmth, something more. Maybe she wouldn't admit it yet, but it was there.

When their breathing calmed, he nudged over alongside her, wrapped his arms around her. His lips were against her temple when he spoke. "I like this place you have here. I got just a little look around when I came in."

"Marisel said she introduced you to her group. She said the girls had you blushing."

"I'll deny that to my dying day."

She chuckled. "That's what you're going with? All right. I'll back you up."

He grinned his appreciation. "So you deliver babies here. What else? What is Marisel's group about?"

"We do a lot of our care in groups, like prenatal visits, for example. The girls get so much more out of it—sharing their experiences, joys, sorrows. So much affects their lives, their pregnancies. Much more than can normally be dealt with in a typical prenatal visit.

"Some of the groups that began for prenatal care continued as a sort of support group. The girls bonded and stuck by each other. We developed other groups, too, in order to reach girls who weren't pregnant, or were between pregnancies.

"We don't do much to lead them, mostly they belong to the girls. We're open to all topics—boys, sex, abuse, families, school, gangs. Largely, we're just giving them the space to meet."

He dipped his nose into her hair, taking pleasure in her scent.

"Our birth rooms are upstairs—two of them, with a sitting room. Marisel and her daughter and grandson have rooms up there, too."

"They live here?"

"Um-hmm. The daughter, Lilibeth, found herself pregnant at sixteen. Marisel had just lost her job, lost their apartment. She brought Lili here and begged for a job. I gave them the extra rooms we had upstairs, and they just kind of stayed on. Marisel works here now and Lilibeth a little bit, too. We have a drop-in daycare that she organizes—it's here on this floor, in the back. We have a little playground out in the courtyard."

He lifted up to look at her. "Drop in daycare. So no one ever has an excuse to leave a baby alone in an apartment."

She tipped her head back to meet his eyes. He let her find what was there, then he kissed her. "I'm in love with a do-gooder."

She paled, her voice laced with nerves. "You're not in love, Cooper."

He pulled her closer, burrowing her into his chest. He took a deep breath and forced himself to have hope. "Okay, then. I've got the hots for a do-gooder."

She pushed back a bit, a mix of annoyance and amusement in her eyes, a blush on her cheeks. "I'm not a crusader, I'm just doing what I can do. This is the best I can make of what I am. I doubt it's different from you—the decision to do the right thing where you can. If everyone did just that much, we'd all be better off, don't you think?"

He held her face to keep eye contact. "Yes, I do. I'm not

criticizing, baby. I'm very impressed with what you've built here. I'm very impressed with you." He swung around to sit up, pulled her up, too. He slid his arm around her shoulder and snugged her close.

"What you do with your life is way different than any woman I've been involved with before. It's very strong and, well, it's like the whole midwife thing."

"You're not involved with me. And what's the whole midwife thing?"

In his mind, he let out a sigh. "Well, you know...a midwife makes me think of a woman with some power—a kind of witchy power."

"Witchy. Uh-huh."

"Also a little earthy."

"Earthy."

"Yeah. Like the kind of woman who wouldn't mind a guy admiring her rack."

"Her...rack."

He bit back a smile at her indignant tone. "Earthy, a little witchy—it's an enticing but somewhat intimidating combination. I imagine a fair number of men are put off by it."

She stood and stepped away from him, stuck her fists in the pockets of her jeans and gave him a dry look. "Really? I can't say I've noticed."

He stood, too, and stepped close. He could see it was her temper that made her stand her ground. "You're twenty-eight, right, single? I don't seem to be fighting my way through a line of guys to see you." He was enjoying himself, but he had to work to keep his eyes from going to that photo of the man with his arm around her.

When she spoke her tone was chilly, but the twinkle that lit her eyes made him nearly certain he hadn't gone too far. "You're not seeing me."

"Yes, I am. Tomorrow, in fact. I'll pick you up at your place at eight."

He kissed her and allowed himself the pleasure of running his hand over her bottom. He gave it a little squeeze. "Get that baby out soon so you can get some sleep. You should still take it easy."

He was gratified by the confusion he saw in her face and ducked out before she found her voice.

CHAPTER SIX

Sylvia didn't want to think about whether Cooper's instructions to "get that baby out" had anything to do with the blessedly quick birth that followed. She knew well that health care workers who took care of laboring women were a notoriously superstitious lot, attributing wild powers to full moons, changes in barometric pressure and a creative list of jinxes.

She'd rather give credit to the confident, trusting attitude and good, positive family support the young woman had brought to her labor. On the other hand, it seemed not the least bit impossible that, if Cooper said a baby should come out fast, the baby would have the good sense to comply. The man seemed to have a certain power himself.

Whatever forces were at work, she was done a little after two o'clock. She was very grateful for it, having found that her healing body was still short on stamina. Too tired to risk the drive home, she curled up with a blanket on her office couch. She caught Cooper's scent there, and, irresistibly, the memory of his warm, strong arms enveloped her. Feeling safe and snug, she slept deeply.

But it was back when she woke—the fear that had wrapped itself around her injured heart the day her father died. She'd had the dream again, the one that sneaked up on her periodically to remind her that her heart had not yet healed. In it, she reached for her father's bloodied arms, smearing her pretty pink party dress in crimson, while he drifted further and further away from her.

Lurching from the couch to the bathroom, she set the shower. She stripped and stepped in, letting the heat hit her full blast. She lifted her face to the spray. The water soothed, washing away tears before she had to admit they were there.

She dressed in the extra change of clothes she kept in the office for just such nights. Feeling fresh if a bit shaken, she went to the kitchen. Marisel was there, watching her carefully while they had coffee. Sylvia gave her a weak smile, exceedingly thankful when her friend was content to chat quietly about last night's birth and the day ahead. They had a quiet clinic morning. They saw a few patients, then Marisel ran a group and Sylvia worked in her office. She'd completed an evaluation for a medical student who'd done some clinical work at the birth center and was grinding through a grant application for an expansion of the drop-in daycare when Marisel knocked at the door.

"Someone here to see you, Sylvie."

She closed her document, surprised to see it was after eleven. She went to the door of her office, surprised again at the identity of her visitor.

The man was tall, broad shouldered, and physically imposing. Attractive braids neatly adorned his head and ended in beads dangling slightly at his neck. His eyes were sharp, his smile engaging. Instinctively, Sylvia mistrusted it.

He extended his hand. "I'm Noah Parsons."

Sylvia put her hand in his, aware that his clasp was a little warmer, a little tighter and longer than a formality. "Sylvia Huston. I recognize you, Councilman, from the newspaper."

"Please call me Noah."

She nodded, waiting. When he waited better, she invited him into her office.

He surveyed the room then gestured to the couch. "Sit, please. I know you were injured last week. You must still need rest."

"Thank you. I'm doing very well."

He smiled, but gestured again to the couch. And held the gesture until she reluctantly complied. She liked it even less when he pulled a chair up close to face her. He sat, leaned forward with his elbows on his knees, his hands clasped almost piously. He gave her an earnest, caring look, but Sylvia was aware that he'd maneuvered her, carefully placing himself in the position of power. She was afraid he might take her hand in his again, and sat back as far into the couch as she could.

"I'm glad to hear you're feeling better. Frankly, I was surprised to learn you were back to work. I checked on your condition while you were in the hospital. Your injury was serious."

Sylvia smiled slightly, wondering why his apparent concern made her so edgy. She reminded herself that the man was a politician, that his interest wasn't personal. "I'm fine. Thank you, again."

He held her gaze for a minute, then nodded. "If you've read about me in the paper, perhaps you've seen that I take seriously the grievous harm done by violence in our community. I make it a point to visit each and every victim of any act of violence that occurs in my ward."

"Your efforts are commendable. I've followed the progress of your town meetings. I like how you've given the people here a voice."

"Yes, it's an effective forum. Yet, I find the most benefit when I meet with my constituents one on one. There is less grandstanding that way, a greater opportunity for an honest exchange of ideas."

Sylvia mentally rolled her shoulders, hoping she was misreading his signals. "You put remarkable effort into your position."

Hope died with his next words. "It's no hardship when the one involved is as lovely as you."

"Thank you. I feel compelled to tell you that I'm not your constituent. I work here, but I vote in another ward."

He smiled indulgently. "I won't hold that against you. I'm told you do very impressive work here. I'd like to hear more."

She stood and smiled brightly, falsely. "I'd be happy to show you around. We do tours regularly, too, if you'd like to join one. We have an open house every first Sunday afternoon."

He came to his feet quickly, closing her in before she could step around him. He lifted his hand, stroked a finger down her cheek, then pressed it against her jaw, tilting her face to his. "I was thinking of a more personal setting. I wonder if you'd join me for dinner tonight."

She took his hand and firmly pushed it away. Obviously, subtlety was wasted. "I'm sorry, I'm already committed." Cooper's plan mattered not at all; she'd have lied without a qualm.

He turned his hand to capture hers. He squeezed and she felt a threat in it. "Tomorrow night, then."

She shook her head. "I'm on call again. I never schedule

a meeting when I'm on call, when I can't give the matter my full attention."

A meeting instead of a date. His eyes told her he'd seen through her strategy and that it wouldn't work. This time the pressure on her hand was overtly painful. "Ah, well. Another time, then." He turned and strode out.

Sylvia leaned back against the wall, deliberately calming her breathing, trying to dispel the sense of menace he'd left behind.

She still felt unsteady two hours later as she sat across a table from her mother. She attributed her emotional instability to the lingering effects of her injury. For sure, the dream about her father's death never visited her now unless she was under unusual stress. She used that evidence to try to convince herself she'd overreacted to Noah Parson's visit. She'd not yet succeeded. Even her mother's warm hug didn't settle her.

The Friday lunch crowd at Mr. Sam's thinned; it would be a couple hours before the dinner rush started. Their waitress had had time to sit and chat for a minute when she brought their linguine and clams.

Now they were alone. Her mother looked gently but intensely into her eyes, and said, "I like him."

"Cooper Billings? He's overbearing and pushy. He thinks he can control everything, everyone."

Katherine smiled, a knowing, someday-you-might-be-as-wise-as-I-am smile that annoyed Sylvia more than usual. "Yes, of course. He's a cop, isn't he? And you're falling in love with him."

The fear clutched, compressing her heart. She shook her head, put her fork down.

Katherine took her hand, sharing a mother's warmth against the chill that gripped her. "Sylvia, you've never been a coward. You're not wrong to have fears, but you've always faced them. You went to midwifery school. You built Tynie's Place. You deliver babies, knowing that each birth could turn into an emergency in a minute. Those things take courage, every day."

"I can't do it, Mama. I'm not going to love him."

"You don't always have a choice about these things, honey."

"I have a choice about this. I just didn't have a choice about papa—"

Katherine drew back, taking her warmth with her.

Sylvia flushed, rubbing her hands over her face. "I'm sorry."

"No. Go on. I didn't realize—you're angry with me about your father, aren't you?"

"No, of course I'm not. How could I be?"

"You are. Tell me."

Sylvia fought tears. She turned her head to watch out the window, noting the various characters hurrying in and out of Barnes & Noble, all bundled against the gray cold. She looked back at her mother, reached for her hand. "If you loved him—" Her mother blanched. "I'm sorry. I know you loved him, so much. So I don't understand how you could let him go out there every day. Out there where..."

Katherine's face lined with grief. "Out there where he could be killed. Where he was killed." She lifted a shoulder. "He was on the job when I met him, when I fell in love with him, when I married him. It was who he was. How could I ask him to change that?

"Think of this. Your job can be hard to live with—you work long hours, all night sometimes. It's physically demanding and sometimes emotionally draining. You live by a pager and when it goes off, you have to go—there's no arguing with it. Not every man can live with that. What if Cooper asked you to give it up?"

Sylvie shook her head. "I could never. It's too..."

"It's too important? Yes. And it's what you are."

"I'm not saying I would ask him to give up being a cop. I'm saying I have a choice about loving him, and I'm not going to do it."

"Do you know, Sylvia, I've had no regrets. I would regret this, though, if losing your father keeps you from finding your happiness."

"You don't really believe that, Mom, do you? That there's only one man I could be happy with, and, if he happens to be a cop, well, I just have to live with it?"

"It doesn't really matter what I believe, does it? It's what you believe that counts. More important, it's what your heart feels."

Her heart. That was what was giving her trouble. She

rubbed a hand over the pain there as she turned to watch out the window again.

By Friday morning they'd gotten lucky. Thursday night Emilio had picked up Rashad's trail and followed him to a meet with a confirmed member of the Plymouth Rocks. That was enough for a warrant. Rashad's car got them prints. An old, poorly executed breaking and entering attempt gave them a match: Antwan Taylor.

Friday afternoon, they broke into Antwan's apartment.

But they were too late. He was already dead.

Emilio and Cooper conferred with homicide at the scene. It looked like payback from the Kings for the hit on Alejandro. Except that there were no signs of a break-in. Except that music videos, now muted, still played on BET. Except that Antwan sat in his easy chair, looking comfortable and relaxed but for the two slugs in his skull. There was an open can of beer on a table next to him and another by the sagging couch.

The partners left the apartment, exchanging anxious glances. Something different was happening.

Friday evening, a seventeen-year-old Hispanic boy was gunned down. Bleeding, barely breathing, he was dumped on the front steps of Tynie's Place.

The birth center was dark, closed down for the weekend. Marisel was there, quiet in her own apartment. Until the police pounded on the door, she hadn't even been aware that Tynie's Place was once again the focus of violence. The call about the shooting victim had come from someone on the street.

She said they'd had a quiet day with no one in labor. Sylvia and the rest of the staff had gone home early.

Cooper called Sylvia's home, but there was no answer. He left a message telling her it didn't look hopeful for their date.

Cooper and Emilio assisted at the scene then followed family members to the hospital. It was too late to help; the young man died in the ambulance and efforts to resuscitate in the ED failed.

They would face a roomful of weeping women: the boy's mother, grandmother, aunts, sisters. Always it was the women who grieved. They would all bitterly shed tears, some quietly, some loudly and with attitude.

They stopped and spoke with the ED attending before they went to the family waiting room. They didn't expect to learn much from that source, but the short interview was routine and expected. The young physician had the desire, and the right, to make clear that he and his staff had done all they could do, that there had been no hope for the young man. That there were many bullets, more than one of which had inflicted fatal damage.

Cooper listened with most of his attention. He heard the wailing from the waiting room, accepted the burden it would be to approach the women there. Their anger and bitterness would soon be targeted on Emilio and him.

He looked through the glass door, assessing as the doc finished his report. His heart leapt when he caught a glimpse of long brown hair gleaming gold. Immediately he thought he was mistaken. He'd been thinking of Sylvia, worried for her, since the call had come in. She'd been on his mind and he was sure that accounted for the surge in his pulse when he saw that hair. Then his feet took him a step closer and he knew it was Sylvie.

She had her arm around a weeping woman. She was there supporting the family. He fought back a primal urge to push through the door, throw his woman over his shoulder, and carry her to safety. She might not understand yet that she was his woman or accept the need he had to keep her safe, but he vowed that she would. Soon.

The woman in her arms was young, a girl, really. She sobbed, collapsed against Sylvie's chest. Cooper absently heard his partner thank the ED doctor, then Emilio touched his arm and walked with him to the roomful of women. He saw then that the girl was very pregnant and knew her child would be born without a father.

Emilio scanned the room and then nudged Cooper in the direction of the woman who appeared to be the victim's mother. The gathering silently parted as they approached her. Her face was ravaged. A woman on either side of her held an arm in support. A boy of eight or nine had his arms circled around her waist and one of her hands held his head pressed against her. But she lifted herself up, held her head high to face them.

Emilio spoke. "Investigators Billings and Navarre, ma'am."

The woman met Emilio's eyes, then Cooper's. "I am Sandra Andujar. My son Tomas is dead."

Emilio nodded. "I'm sorry, Mrs. Andujar. We will do whatever we can to make this easier for you tonight."

Sandra Andujar looked away, rubbed at her eyes with a crumpled hankie.

Cooper spoke next. "We've been assigned to investigate the shooting, ma'am."

She looked back at him, eyes empty. "You won't find him. You won't find who did this."

Cooper accepted the words, and the implied blame. "Yes, ma'am. We will."

The woman shook her head. "It won't matter, anyway. It won't bring Tomas back."

Emilio spoke next, quietly. "It will matter. It will matter to other mothers. To sisters and aunts." He looked down at the boy crying against his mother. "It will matter to other brothers."

Mrs. Andujar clutched at the boy who clung to her. Emilio gently insinuated himself at her side and walked her to a seat. He sat beside her and began asking about her son.

Cooper drew aside the woman Emilio had displaced and got a small part of the story from her. Tomas, her nephew, had been unemployed, a high-school dropout. He'd been a good boy, but had nothing to do with himself. He spent more and more time on the street. He might have been involved with a gang, but the aunt would not or could not say for sure. She did say the young man had become bitter and hostile, no longer comfortable to be around.

Sylvia had met Cooper's eyes when he entered the room. They'd watched each other for just a moment, then both had returned to their work. Sylvia had calmed the pregnant girl now, leading her to a sofa and encouraging her to lie down and rest. She went out to the nurses' station and returned with a blanket and pillow. She tucked in the girl and then left again.

When she came back, she had a cup of coffee. She nodded at Emilio and knelt beside Sandra Andujar, placing the warm cup in the woman's hands, wrapping her fingers around it and holding them there. Sandra distractedly nodded her thanks.

Sylvia rubbed the back of the boy who snuggled in his mother's lap. "Come on, Mateo. Let's go find a candy bar. I know where the best machines are here."

She walked near Cooper as she passed through the room, the boy's hand in hers. When she was near enough, Cooper put out a hand to stop her. Gently holding her at the shoulder, he looked into her face and saw the deep sadness. For a moment he pulled her to him, held her against him for comfort, pressed his lips to her temple. When he let her go, she gave him a small smile. Before she walked away, he touched his lips to hers. "I'll see you tomorrow."

He watched her go, then turned to one of the younger women—this one Tomas's cousin. He and Emilio had a long night ahead of them.

They worked into the early morning hours. They spoke to each of the family members present at the hospital, then walked Mrs. Andujar through the sad task of identifying Tomas's body. That done, they left the hospital and hit the streets.

Dawn was just taking the edge off the night sky when they sat in Cooper's driveway, engine idling. They were quiet as they watched the dark lift.

Finally, Cooper spoke. "It seems very simple. Antwan Taylor doesn't like his sister getting messed with, takes a shot at Alejandro. That pisses off the Kings, they take out Antwan. The Rocks get revenge by killing Tomas Andujar."

"And we got a gang war."

"Yeah."

"Seems simple." Emilio chewed on it for a while. "Doesn't feel so simple, does it?"

"Nope."

"Why not?"

Cooper laid his head back, closed his eyes. "Antwan was sittin' in his easy chair."

"None of the Kings were strutting about the hit. They weren't complaining, but no one was taking credit."

"Someone's pulling a power play in the Rocks, said no to Antwan's plan to do Alejandro."

"And Antwan dissed him."

"So this someone takes out Antwan. He's with the Rocks, comes to have a chat with his boy. Drinks a beer, then caps him in his easy chair."

Cooper continued the thought. "It's safe to assume the Kings will take the blame for it. So he pops Tomas Andujar to keep fires stoked."

"What does it get him? If he wants control of the Rocks, how does a gang war help him?"

"Right. If he's trying to establish his power, then Antwan's death has to look like what it was—discipline. Punishment for defying the council."

"Maybe somebody didn't get the message. Antwan's buddy, someone close to him. Acted on Tomas before word got out."

Cooper looked over at his partner. "Then he'll be our next dead guy."

Emilio rubbed the back of his neck. "So who's the someone? Who's trying to take over?"

"It's Parsons."

"You mean, you want it to be Parsons."

"It is, Emilio. It makes sense. He lived high in Baltimore, had a hell of a bankroll." He paused. "Baltimore's one of the largest East Coast heroin ports."

"And you're going to tell me that heroin has been making a comeback in the city."

"It's true."

"If you've got the source, then developing a gang to put it on the street would be a smart way to market it."

"He's smart."

"That he is."

A few hours' sleep didn't make the situation appear any prettier. Fighting a feeling of doom, Cooper took a break for football practice while Emilio set up a meeting.

Fear of escalating violence led to a good turnout. Representatives of neighborhood watch groups, local church pastors, and counselors from the community centers joined the loose group of police officers tackling gang issues. Inevitably, Noah Parsons blessed them with his presence.

"Who invited him?" Cooper muttered, trying to shrug Emilio's restraining hand from his shoulder.

"Settle down. You know we're not going to give a party without him hearing about it."

Emilio called the meeting to order, requesting that the group keep its focus on practical, immediate measures. Philosophical discussions about the root causes of gang violence would have to wait for another day, another forum, he argued.

Parsons would have none of it. Recognizing a bully pulpit when he saw one, he took the opportunity to extol his own sincere commitment to the safety of the citizenry while lambasting the police for their failure to stop the violence. A television press crew had followed him in, recording while he preened in the spotlight.

Diplomatically, Emilio thanked the councilman for his remarks and asked that further addresses to the press take place outside the meeting area. Parsons moved to a corner of the room where he demonstrated his importance by making cell calls and conferencing with his aides.

Emilio coordinated break out groups to tackle specific issues. An hour later, they reconvened to finalize a plan.

They developed a blueprint for increasing police presence in the neighborhood surrounding Tynie's Place. They laid out a strategy to disrupt drug markets in the area by altering local traffic patterns. And they identified measures to help promote a zero-tolerance atmosphere for gang activity in the neighborhood.

Cooper was content with the outcome of the meeting. The police were motivated to do their part. More importantly, the civilians were committed and clearly understood that police efforts were only a part of the solution.

His satisfaction with the small success of the meeting soured when Parsons, waiting until the room cleared, approached him at the exit.

"Officer Billings."

Cooper looked down at his shoulder, where the man's hand brought him to a stop. When he looked up, Parsons dropped his hand and took a step back. Cooper matched that step, thrusting out his chest a bit.

Parsons gathered himself. "I wonder when the force will quit dodging its responsibilities for the safety of the people. Once again you've place the burden on the city's poor and disenfranchised."

Emilio stepped between them, using his shoulder to hold Cooper back. "I'm sure you're aware, Councilman, that every city in the country is dealing with the same problems. There are limits to what the force can do, unless you're advocating a police state. We're on the street. We do what we can."

Parsons ignored him, keeping his gaze on Cooper. "I notice that what you can do improves a lot when it's a pretty white girl who gets hurt."

Cooper surged forward. He made a grab for Parsons's coat, but Emilio blocked it.

Parsons gloated. "Ms. Huston and I had nice chat this morning. She's a lovely young woman. We plan to see each other again."

This time Cooper wouldn't be stopped. He took a fistful of the man's coat, put his face in his, and growled. "Stay away from her, Noah."

Ever aware of the chance for a photo op, Parsons glanced toward the door, clearly wishing the camera crew was still there. "Take your hands off me, Billings, or your own partner will have to testify against you on assault charges."

"When I assault you, you'll know it, Councilman." Cooper held him for another moment, then let him go with a small shove. "Don't ever touch her, Noah. I mean it."

Parsons shrugged his coat back into place, mean amusement glinting in his eyes. "Her little birth center is in my ward. That puts Tynie's Place, and her, under my protection. I wouldn't want any harm to come to either."

Emilio went by Tynie's Place. The first floor was dark. He could see a distant light through a second floor window, coming from the back of the building. There was a bell alongside the door, so he rang it.

In a few moments Marisel opened the door. He nodded. "*Hola, Senora.*"

She did not smile, stood just inside the door. She answered as he had begun, in Spanish. "*Detectivo.*"

He was not encouraged, though he would have been hard pressed to explain exactly why he was there. "I wondered how your patient was doing—Tomas Andujar's girlfriend." It was weak and he knew it.

She perused his face before she answered. "Elisabeth. She's doing okay." She paused, her eyes still on him. "Would you like to come in? I'll make a cup of tea."

He nodded again and entered as she stepped back. He knew she had rooms upstairs, wondered if she had a kitchen there, too, but followed her quietly to the kitchen on the main floor, the one used for the birth center.

She turned on lights as she went, then motioned him to a chair at the large, oval table. She started the heat under an old-fashioned teakettle. "We brought Elisabeth here last night. We have space so her family and Tomas's could gather. Then we gave her something to help her sleep. She woke up late this morning and her family took her home. She is due in a couple weeks. It will be a hard, sad labor for her."

"Is this kind of stress dangerous during pregnancy?"

She shrugged a little as she set mugs on the table. "Sylvie could tell you better. Women survive a lot of bad things during pregnancy—and their babies, too. Elisabeth, though, she doesn't have much. Her family has not been so good for her. Mrs. Andujar is a better mother to her than her own."

"Will she stay involved in the girl's life, do you think?"

"We hope she will. It's the kind of woman she is. This baby is Tomas's first—only, now—child. That will mean something to Sandra Andujar."

They were quiet for a moment. She sat as she finished with the tea. They both held the mugs to warm their hands before they sipped.

"You and Sylvia do good work here."

She shrugged again, a motion that took his eyes to her shoulder, the soft curls that rested there. "You ask Sylvie, she'll just say we're doing what we can do, what is the right thing to do. But she's built a kind of magic here."

When she fell quiet, he lifted his eyes to hers, where they held.

"She can change peoples' lives. She changed mine."

He watched her, kept his hands on his cup of tea even as they seemed to want to lift, to touch. "I believe people change their own lives."

She smiled a little, her eyes softening. "*Si*, maybe so. But sometimes angels help. To me, Sylvie is an angel."

They watched each other for a moment, then her smile widened. "I think maybe your friend Investigator Billings thinks she is an angel, too, no?"

"*Si.*"

Their smiles lingered. He reached across the table to touch her fingers where they curved around the cup. "I think more than one *angel* works here."

CHAPTER SEVEN

She looked like an angel when she opened the door to him. Each time he saw her, the traces of the physical trauma she had experienced faded more. Each time she looked more beautiful.

He was pleased to see she'd dressed for dinner. He'd called her before he left the station, telling her he'd pick her up in an hour for dinner. He'd not made it a polite request. He knew he'd pushed her and was more relieved than he wanted to admit that she'd allowed it.

He stood at the door for a moment, enjoying the look of her. She was dressed simply, comfortably, and, to his delight, damned sexily. She wore a stretch black velvet top. It clung nicely to her curves, the wrap neckline drawing his eyes to an enticing glimpse of breast. A silver chain glimmered at her neck and a garnet pendant dangled just there, teasing. Her skirt was long and draped, swinging gently just above her ankles. It was a crimson velvety print that shimmered with her movement but also suggestively caressed her body. Her feet were bare in her shoes, and he knew there was nothing between the velvet of her skirt and the smoothness of her legs. The shoes were flat but feminine, black slippers with a cutout at the arch. He could imagine sliding his fingers in there, stroking.

Earthy. Witchy. Sexy. He was done for.

When his eyes found his way back to hers, she had a brow arched. He hoped he was seeing a little indulgent humor there. He cleared his throat, tried not to think about whether he was blushing.

He stepped through the door, to her. He put his arms around her and pulled her to him. She slid her arms around his shoulders and rested her head against him. He touched his lips to her hair. "How's your patient?"

"She's okay. We kept her the night at the birth center,

just to watch her."

"Good." He stayed quiet, not exactly sure of himself.

"I was glad when you came to the hospital last night. I'd wondered if you would."

He tightened his arms a little.

"It was better, once you were there."

The pleasure of that shuddered through him. He pushed a little, taking her back into the room. He lifted one hand from her to swing the door shut behind him. When his hand moved back to her, it gripped.

She let out a little sound. Desire, he thought, tinged with fear. He gave thanks for the one, damned the other. He pulled her hard against him. His hands slid over her, drawn by the velvet and the heat beneath it. He brought them up her sides, where his thumbs could stroke along the outer curve of her breasts. Then he slipped them behind her, bringing her in so he could feel the firm rounds of her breasts press against his chest.

He sank his head down to where she nestled into him. Her breath was hot, honeyed. "Let me have your mouth."

She whimpered but her fingers clutched at the suit jacket over his shoulders, inside the woolen overcoat he'd left open. He waited, breathing hard, for what seemed like an eternity.

At last she lifted her head until their lips met. They just touched at first while both drew several breaths. Then, with a moan, he took her.

He moved one hand to her nape to hold her. With his mouth he pillaged, stroking, nipping, grazing with lips and teeth and tongue. When he slid into her, to taste her, she quivered, then met his tongue with hers.

Home, he thought, *this is home*. He trailed his hand down her spine, kneading and pressing. He followed her spine to its base and slipped lower still, pressing his fingers into the crevice there until she groaned.

"Cooper."

The tone was pleading, but he wasn't sure what she was asking. He considered whether he had it in him to pull back. His hand slid around her bottom and squeezed there while he thought about it, bringing her firmly against his erection.

Her breath caught and her body tensed. Before it was too late, he raised his head. He loosened his grip, allowing a little space between their bodies. He took his other hand from be-

hind her neck, moved it to her jaw to lift her face to his. He
waited until her eyes met his.

"I want you, Sylvie."

A little jolt shivered through her. She dropped her head,
tried to burrow into his shoulder, but he held her with his
hand on her jaw. He stroked her lips with his thumb, followed with his mouth, gently. "Will you let me have you?"

She shuddered again but after a moment her lips moved
against his. They lingered in the kiss, touching softly, breathing in synchrony.

"Will you, baby?"

On a sigh, she said it. "Yes."

He closed his eyes and took a few breaths without moving. He took her into his heart, felt strengthened, whole. He
kissed her once more. "Thank you, love."

Then he gave her a pat on the butt. "Let's go."

She looked up at him a bit blankly. "Let's go?"

"I promised you dinner."

"Dinner?"

It turned out he got a lot of pleasure in leaving her
stunned. He couldn't hold back the grin, watching her shake
her head, trying to catch up. "Yeah. Food. Come on."

She let out a sigh, ran her hand through her hair in a way
that left it sweetly tousled. She gave him a look that said she
was onto the fun he was having. "Okay."

He helped her with her coat, snugged her into it, then
used it to pull her against him. "One thing..." He put his lips on
hers, not gently, but taking. "All through dinner..." He thrust
his tongue into her, took some more. "I'll be thinking of everything I'm going to do to you when I bring you back here."

She shot him another speaking look and he laughed as
he followed her out the door. He considered the sound of his
own laughter. Joy. That was something.

Cooper didn't just think of what he was going to do to
her, he told her. He sat across from her, at a table so small
that their knees touched. So small that he could easily reach
her, stroke her fingers, her cheek, her hair. With each touch
he told her how it would be to lie with him. He told her more
with his eyes, the heat there flaring as he lost track of the
conversation while he gazed at her lips, her breasts. And he
spoke of it to her, hotly, bluntly.

They touched wineglasses and sipped, the Merlot glowing ruby red in candlelight, its taste erotic. He distracted her with questions about the birth center. As she answered, he toyed with her fingers, rubbing with his thumbnail at the pad of her forefinger.

She was telling him about her benefactor, the man who'd left her the money to buy Tynie's Place, when he interrupted.

"I'm going to put my tongue on you, taste you. Everywhere. There's not an inch of you I'll miss. Not. One. Inch."

Sylvia's breath shuddered. She closed her eyes, grasping to keep a thought in her head. When she opened her eyes again he watched her.

"Go on," he said.

She pulled herself back to the story. "His name was Angelo Lorenzo. He was an engineer at Kodak for fifty years. He never retired, just kept going to his office every day of his life.

"I met him when I was a nursing student. He'd had a stroke. He could still speak, but he could no longer walk or really care for himself. His doctors recommended nursing home care.

"He refused. I helped him set up home health aides and physical therapy. I visited him almost every day for the next year. I held his hand when he died, at home in his own bed, as he wanted.

"He'd never married, had no family in this country—he'd immigrated when he was seventeen. He lived very frugally in a small apartment near the Kodak plant. He saved a small fortune, and he left it to me in his will.

"Over that year he heard my dreams of a birth center. He knew what I would do with the money."

Cooper nodded. He took her hand and dipped her forefinger into her wine. He took it to his mouth and sipped, then suckled, drawing in. His tongue brushed at the most sensitive spot, where his thumbnail had just been stroking. His teeth scraped. He let her go only when the waiter arrived with their meals.

Sylvia sighed in relief at the diversion. Her body thrummed, strung tightly as harp strings. Since they met, he'd seduced her mercilessly. Her mind, maybe even her heart, could resist him, but her body had long ago become his. It filled her with fear, the way he could make her want.

She had some small experience with men. There'd been

a law student while she was in nursing school, a resident during graduate school. She'd thought she was in love and it had been pleasant to be with them, to be held, touched.

It had been nothing at all like what Cooper did to her. He made her burn, made her hot and needy. Made desire override her fear, her better sense.

He was a cop. She reminded herself every time she saw him, every time she thought of him, and now, when she looked at him, wanting him. She would never love a cop; she knew too much already about pain. It became a litany: she would never love him.

"Taste this."

She came back to him. He was holding a piece of his steak to her lips, using his own fork. His face was all innocence, but the words had been laden with sensuality, with sex.

She opened her lips and took the steak. He watched intently as she chewed. He didn't speak until she swallowed.

"I keep imagining having my mouth on your breast, sucking your nipple."

She gripped the edge of the table, conquering with effort the urge to bolt. He watched her until she calmed then returned to his steak, though his eyes seldom left her.

After a few moments, he motioned to her plate. "Your pasta looks good."

The twinkle in his eyes steadied her, nearly making her smile. His dinner was almost gone. "You want some?"

"I'll take a taste, but you need to eat." He waited as she took a couple bites. "You'll need the energy."

She felt the blush on her cheeks. She knew it deepened when he took a forkful himself and then chewed it slowly, provocatively. He nodded to her plate and she kept eating, barely tasting the food.

He took a last sip of his wine then slipped his hand under the table. She felt his fingers on her knee; after a minute they began moving, slowly rucking up her skirt. Soon they were on her naked leg, stroking the inside of her knee.

"The velvet of your skirt rubbing against your skin. I've been thinking of that all night."

Sylvie fought to keep her breath steady. She nearly jumped when the waiter approached. She began to shake her head when he asked about dessert, but Cooper overrode her.

"Crème brulée. One. We'll share."

When they were alone he leaned close to her. He caressed with more heat, moving a little up her thigh. He spoke in a husky whisper. "When I push into you, you'll be hot and wet. You'll scream."

She put her fingers over her lips, stifling a cry. "Cooper," she pleaded.

"I want you. I've made no secret of it. When I have you, when we have each other, it's going to be like nothing we've known before. You know that, don't you?"

She couldn't deny it. His words echoed the thoughts that had only just been in her mind. She couldn't refuse to answer, because he waited, watching, not letting her go with his eyes. She could only say the truth. "Yes. I do."

He nodded, satisfaction more than obvious.

When the waiter came back with their dessert, he waved it away and handed over a card. "Thanks, but we're in a hurry."

He drove her home in silence, not touching her except for gently clasping her hand. Sylvia was thankful for the reprieve, feeling battered by the intensity of his desire, so powerfully expressed. And by her own desire, she had to admit. It was enough to make her tremble, the way he aroused her hunger. Her body was still heated, so sensitized it seemed any touch would cause her to shatter.

He pulled into her driveway and shut off the car. He gazed out the windshield for a minute, then turned to her, his arm resting on the back of his seat. She stayed quiet as his eyes held hers, searching. Finally he spoke. "I saw Noah Parsons this afternoon. He said he'd seen you."

Sylvia weighed his words. His tone was bland but there was an undercurrent she couldn't interpret. "Yes. He came to my office. He wanted to express his concern about my injury."

"He told me you were planning to see him again."

She caught her breath, offended first by Parsons's gall and then by Cooper's. He lifted his hand before she could start listing her objections.

"I figure he's playing me."

She was partly mollified. "Yes. He is."

He nodded, but still watched her carefully. "You know me, at least well enough to know I'd never share."

He'd laid down terms. He was blunt in this, uncompromising. If she couldn't accept that side of his nature, she should get out of the car alone. She considered then discarded that option. Despite her fears, despite her memories, she wanted him in a way that she was compelled to explore. Besides, she couldn't disagree with his sentiment.

She returned his gaze steadily. "Neither would I."

A small smile lightened his expression. "Agreed."

He turned his body, put a hand on the door lever, then looked back to her once more. "One thing, though. I've known Noah a long time. He's dangerous. If he approaches you again, tell me right away."

"That's a request?"

He took a quiet breath. "Yes. Please."

She nodded. "Okay."

Not quite quelling his look of satisfaction, he exited the car. He circled around to open her door but didn't offer his hand to help her out. She understood: she would join him of her own accord.

When she stood, they were separated by the door of the car, a bright red classic GTO that suited him so well she'd laughed when he'd first taken her to it. She imagined that in its day an eight-track tape had blared out vintage rock and that heads had turned to follow it. Just as they would turn to follow the man who drove it. Not so different from now.

She looked up into his face and barely held back a tremor. His passion hadn't diminished. It had merely been banked as he brought her home.

Now he watched her out of eyes that flared, his face drawn in need, and, she perceived, a little tension. He was not sure of her yet.

With good reason, as she was not sure of herself. She was afraid. Fear and desire battled within her. But she was not a coward, and she would not deny the desire.

She knew there was suffering in his need. Compelled to alleviate it, she reached up to touch his face. He groaned and nuzzled her hand. She brushed her thumb over his lips. "Come inside."

Cooper raised he head and searched her eyes, looking for and finding, she knew, consent. He closed his eyes for a moment. When he opened them, he had the look of a warrior.

He pulled her out from behind the car door and slammed it closed. Then, with his hand firmly at the small of her back, he directed her toward her front steps. He took the keys from her hand and opened the door. He ushered her through, closed the door, locked it.

He looked back at the door, gumwood with amber diamond-patterned glass that was repeated throughout her house. "Here," he said, as he pushed her to the wall beside the door. "Now."

He tore off his overcoat and tossed it in the direction of the entrance table. He took hers, too, sending it after his, appearing to have not a care that both coats slid to a heap on the floor. All that seemed to matter was that he was against her, pressing her bodily into the wall at her back, putting his mouth on hers.

His hands held her face, turning it to the angle that gave him best access. His thumb pressed on her jaw until she opened for him and then he took her.

His tongue probed her, tasting, taking. It thrust into her, in a rhythm her body recognized, anticipated. She felt her breasts tighten against the raw silk of his jacket. Their breathing was rough, needy.

He pressed solidly against her, thigh to thigh, his hardness sinking into her center. She moaned in desire, raising her hands to grasp greedily at his hair.

His fingers left her face. They trailed down her neck then rested over her collarbones. Still ravaging her mouth, he moved his hands between them until they covered her breasts. She struggled for breath, each labored inhalation lifting her breasts more into his possession.

"Yes," he said, encouraging her. "Arch like that. God, yes."

Driven to comply, she strained to fill his hands. He groaned his satisfaction. For a moment, his held his taut body still.

Then she felt a change in his touch on her breasts. His fingers curled, slipping inside the velvet of her top, catching the edges of lace underneath. He pulled down, rasping knuckles over her nipples, baring her breasts.

For the first time he let go of her mouth. He pulled back enough for their eyes to meet, then further so that when he lowered his gaze, her breasts were displayed for him. She shuddered, watching him view her.

Cooper's hands moved over her, stroking, gently squeezing. "You're so beautiful." There was awe in his voice. "Look,"
he instructed. "Watch."

Her breath caught as she lowered her gaze. She watched
as he circled her breasts with thumb and fingers, his skin dark
against hers, looking strong and competent, proclaiming own-
ership. He lifted her so that her distended nipples jutted out.

Watching intently himself, he leaned forward, rubbing
against her so the rough silk of his jacket chafed her rigid
peaks. It sent a spasm of heat into her core. Within seconds,
it wasn't enough for her. Her next moan was a command and
he read it perfectly.

He moved his fingers to grasp her nipples, tugging, pulling. He swallowed her cry when he took her mouth again.
Their bodies strained.

He freed one breast, taking a hand to pull up the hem of
her skirt. As he bent to strip away the lacy froth of her panties, he put his mouth on her breast, sucking torturously at
her nipple.

Then his hand was under her skirt and she was bare to
him. His fingers found the thatch where her thighs joined and
he stroked. Blood rushed in her head so that she could barely
hear his demand. "Open your legs. Just a little."

She did as he bade, opening herself to him. His fingers
were aggressive, compelling. They found the nub of her center and rubbed at it, nearly taking her over. Then they ex-
plored further, discovered her cleft and sank in.

"Hot. Wet." His tongue went to her mouth again, thrust
into her along with his fingers. Frantic, she tore at his shirt to
get her hands inside, to touch his heated skin.

For a moment, his hands were gone from her and she
understood he was freeing himself. When it was done, his
hands came back under her skirt. They brought folds of velvet with them as they rode up her thighs. They circled
around the backs, almost to her buttocks. Then they separated and lifted her, imprisoning her between his hard body
and the wall, spreading her legs wide so she was open, entirely vulnerable.

He raised her enough that he could put his mouth back on
her breasts. He nipped, sucking hard. Then he lowered her
until she felt him press at her opening. He thrust, impaling.

She screamed.

Screamed again as he thrust a second time, and then again. He filled her, stretched her. With the next penetration she began to climax, a long shattering wave that rolled over her as he pounded into her.

In a moment, he clutched at her, arching back as he strained into her, emptied into her, a guttural moan escaping his throat.

Sylvia felt his spasms peak and then diminish inside her. He cried out once more as he held her to him.

She closed her eyes as he slowly removed himself and let her slide down until her feet touched the floor again. He held her with his body until her legs could support her weight. He fumbled with his own clothing and then gently rearranged hers until she was covered again. He held her head, pressed his lips against her forehead.

"Stay here, baby. Just a minute. Don't move." He touched his lips to her, then stepped away, leaving her pressed against the wall.

She knew exactly what had happened. She had been branded, made his. His body had imprinted itself on hers, a mating that her flesh would forever recognize. She kept her eyes closed, concentrating on breathing in and out. Wondering if she could accept it. If she could refuse it.

When he left her, he went up the stairs to her bedroom. He turned down the pretty flowered comforter, opened the soft green bed sheets. He lit the candles that were scattered about the room—long tapers in front of the mirror over her dresser, thick, scented cylinders on bedside tables, tea candles in an arrangement at the window.

He draped his suit coat over a chair, slipped out of his shoes and socks. Hesitating only a moment, he took off his shirt, too.

He went back down and stood silently before her. He knew she understood what it had meant, the way he had taken her. He knew she would struggle with the significance of it. There was not a lot he could do to help her with it. He wouldn't apologize for it. But his heart was filled with tenderness for her.

"Come on, baby."

She opened her eyes, kept them at the level of his chest. She raised her arms a little and his heart sang. He lifted her up in his arms, pulled her snugly to his chest. He turned and carried her upstairs.

He liked the way his muscles worked when he carried her, easily up to the task. He had a flash of prehistoric man taking his woman to his cave. He was not uncomfortable with the image.

He set her down next to the bed. Gently, silently, he undressed her. She was quiet, unresisting.

When she was nude, he stepped away from her and slid out of his slacks and boxers. Then he lifted her again and lay down with her on the bed. Partly covering her, he cupped her face. He waited until she lifted her eyes to meet his.

"I love you, Sylvie. There's nothing for it but for us to marry. That's what's between us." He stroked her face when she closed her eyes, reminded himself of how she had given herself to him, opened herself to him. He knew she would never have done so if she didn't love him, even if she might not know it yet.

"I understand that you're not ready. I'll do my best to give you time. But that's where we're headed. I'd ask you not to deceive yourself about that."

A small sound came from her throat and two tears seeped from the corners of her eyes. He put his mouth to them, sipping. "Don't cry, love. Please."

He scattered soft, undemanding kisses over her face, thankful when there were no more tears. His lips circled hers as desire stirred in him again. He fought it down, knowing now that she needed to control what happened between them next.

"I heard Marisel talking to the girls in her group. She told them they should require that boys ask permission to kiss them, touch them. She said it was their right to give it or not."

He took her cheek, turned her face to his. When she opened her eyes he let her see his hunger. He stayed still, letting her know that it was her call.

"I want to kiss your mouth. Will you let me?"

After a moment, she nodded and he let out a quiet sigh. Softly, he pressed his lips to hers. He took a lot of time, stimulating, arousing. On a breath, her mouth opened and she lifted to have more of him.

Her tongue touched his and he followed it back, sinking into her mouth. The kisses became greedy, needy. Her arms circled his neck, holding him to her.

He hardened, pressing himself a bit into the mattress to keep from pushing her. He wondered briefly if he would survive this.

"I want my hands on your breasts. Let me." He was pretty sure he'd failed at making that a question.

"Yes." She arched into him as his hands covered her. "Yes."

He wanted to crow in victory. He'd listened to Marisel's advice with skepticism, thinking that surely there would be no romance left if a man had to ask permission for every liberty. Instead, he found it fired his passion, to have her admit her desire for his touch.

He took her breasts, thumbs stroking her nipples. She ran her hands over his arms, firm where his muscles bunched to hold his weight off of her. Her nails dug in. She writhed beneath him, rising up against his hardness.

"My mouth. I want them in my mouth."

She arched more, offering. He took one and then the other, pulling hard to have the nipple tight in his mouth, tonguing it. She held his head against her, fingernails furrowing down his back. She moaned.

He was close to losing it. It took all his effort to hold back. "Sylvie. I want to touch you. I want my fingers inside you."

"Yes, Cooper."

He rolled a little to her side and pressed his knee up between her legs, opening them. He slid his fingers down, brushing over the curve of her belly, rising over her mound. Then he was at her core, tweaking the small, sensitive nub between his fingers. She cried out as he stroked her, and he was too tempted. "More?"

"Yes." She tilted her pelvis to increase the pressure. He kept touching, stroking until she bucked, going rigid in orgasm.

He grinned, hiding it against her breast while she quieted. He gave her only a minute, then he moved his fingers lower, pressing in.

"You said I could put them inside you."

"No."

"No?" He couldn't resist a single stroke and she arched again.

"Umm—yes."

His two fingers delved into her wet velvet. She felt so tight, he wondered if her scream when he had entered her had been all in pleasure. He stilled his fingers.

She wriggled against him, but still he waited. She opened her eyes, looked at him in question.

"You're so small—I wondered if I'd hurt you."

She shook her head. "I'm not small. I have a pelvis that will—"

She broke off, but he knew where she'd been going. A pelvis that will birth babies easily. That thought burned into him, a primal reaction coiling through him.

He'd taken her, was about to take her again, and had not protected her. Since he was seventeen, he'd never had a woman without protecting her.

This woman would bear his child. His children.

Watching her, he began to stroke her again. She started to turn her head away, but he stopped her with a grunted command. "No. Look at me."

Their gazes held as he pushed his fingers harder into her. She keened out a response, eyes darkening in pleasure. He hadn't hurt her, he wouldn't. Her desire, her needs, matched his own.

"I want to be inside you now." He emphasized that with another hard stroke of his fingers.

Her body quaked. "Yes."

"I want you to watch me when I take you."

"Yes."

"I want to watch you when I make you come."

"Yes."

He took his fingers out of her and put them on her lips, rubbing, opening them. He slipped them into her mouth then followed with his tongue until they shared the taste of her.

He lifted over her, took her hands, threading fingers, and positioned them on either side of her head, tangling in the gold-gleaming strands of her hair.

They watched each other as he slowly penetrated her. Their breathing tightened, their bodies trembled, their clasped hands battled before he began to move.

She arched and started to moan almost immediately. He sank into her, deep, then held her there. Her eyes flashed fire at him.

"Not yet. I want to take you farther."

She squirmed under him, seeking, but still he held her.

"I'm going to make you give me more."

She arched once more, then sank down into the bed. It was not submission, however. Challenge in her eyes, she brought her knees up, then dropped them open, open, cradling him so that his weight carried him deeper into her.

The movement sent a spear of pleasure stabbing through him, threatening his control. Sweat slicked his body as he held himself over her, in her. Unable to resist, he withdrew, nearly completely, so he could sink into her again, inch by inch.

Seated to the hilt, he began to rock. They watched each other as passion flared. When they needed more, he pulled back and then plunged into her, over and over.

Their eyes held until the last second, when ecstasy overtook them and they tumbled over the edge, free falling, together.

Just before sleep took them, he ran his fingers through her hair and turned her to face him. "Sylvie."

Her eyes fluttered, opening for just a second. "Hmm?"

"I didn't use any protection."

She opened her eyes a little more, managed to keep them open. "It's usually better to have this conversation before, rather than after."

"Usually I do. Or rather, I don't, necessarily, but I use a condom. Always."

Her eyes closed again. "That's good."

"Sylvie." He only just kept himself from shaking her.

"Don't worry, the timing isn't right."

"I'm not worried." At least, not about a pregnancy. Her eyes stayed closed, her breathing softened. Giving up, he stroked her cheek and laid his head next to hers. Quietly, he spoke. "I want my baby inside you."

So maybe she wasn't quite asleep. She snuggled into him, whispering into his chest. "Cooper, you're going to break my heart."

Or you mine, he thought. Which was it going to be?

CHAPTER EIGHT

A pager woke them, and they both fumbled at the bed-side table. After a moment of confusion, Cooper realized, first, that he was not in his own bedroom and, second, that it was not his pager blaring.

It was light out—as light as it would get in the gray November of Rochester. They'd slept late. During the night, they'd come together again—twice, maybe, now that he thought of it. Heat, passion, and love, he was sure of it. They slept tangled together, neither willing to let go.

He was ready for this—love, marriage, family. He knew in the back of his mind he'd been seeking exactly this. He was sure he hadn't been desperate. When his engagement ended and he settled in Rochester, he began dating. He found interesting, attractive women. He enjoyed them, took some of them to bed.

He hadn't fallen for any of them.

Now he'd fallen hard. He was happy, certain he wasn't mistaken, certain it was the woman, not his own longings that made him have to have her.

She was warm against him, still in his arms despite the fact that she'd gone from pager to telephone. He tried hard not to listen as she had a conversation about whether the caller's water had broken. To distract himself—something he wanted badly—he began tasting her. He remembered promising to put his tongue everywhere on her, and he thought there were some places he'd missed.

He toyed with her navel until he heard the catch in her voice. She took a handful of his hair and tugged, then swatted at him when he wouldn't be moved.

She made what sounded to him like a hurried plan to meet the woman at the birth center in a couple hours and hung up. She put her hands on him, stroking his hair, his shoulders. He looked up at her and she smiled.

He slid his hand up, nearly circling her breast. "Good morning."

She touched his face, her hand soft against the bristle of his beard. "Good morning. I'm on call today. I've got to go in."

"In two hours, you said." He had her fingers in his mouth now and felt her shudder.

"I need to get some breakfast—"

"I can help with that."

"And shower."

His mouth was hovering over hers now, still suckling on her fingers. "I can *really* help with that."

She laughed until his lips took hers. Their bodies melded, arching into each other as the kiss deepened. After a few minutes, he pulled himself back. He squeezed her bottom. "I'll make the coffee. You start the shower."

He was home in time for the call from Sunday. The informant confirmed Emilio's observation—no one was swaggering, taking credit for the death of either Antwan or Tomas. The Kings were behaving as expected: crowing about revenge, vowing to take war to the streets. But the Rocks were unexpectedly quiet, restrained, Sunday thought. They almost seemed nervous. He couldn't explain it, he said.

Cooper worried over that for a while, then changed the subject. "Hey, what do you know about the birth center, Tynie's Place?"

There was silence on the line, then Sunday spoke quietly. "The midwife walks both sides. Women from the Kings and the Rocks go there. They talk to each other, join groups together. It's like what happens on the streets don't matter so much there."

Cooper wasn't surprised that Sunday knew about Tynie's Place, but hadn't expected him to know about the groups. "What else?"

Over the line he could hear the shrug. The young man knew he'd said too much. "Nothing else."

"Why was Tomas dumped there?"

"I don't know, man. Kinda seems like a warning, don't it?"

Fear slid icy fingers down Cooper's spine. "Is somebody upset with the midwife?"

"I haven't heard anything. Most of the guys think she's okay. She looks at them, you know? Talks to them. Most white women don't do that."

"And she delivers their babies."

"That, too."

Cooper wondered if he heard a softening in Sunday's voice. "I want to know right away if you hear anything about her, anything at all."

Now he was afraid Sunday was trying to interpret what was in his voice.

"You got a thing for the midwife, man?"

"Yeah, I do."

"She's a good woman."

Again, Cooper wondered about Sunday's connection to Tynie's Place. He was pretty sure Sylvia would know Sunday.

He set down the receiver and paced. The conversation verified his and Emilio's suspicions. Something different was happening in the gangs, at least for the Rocks. And maybe even they didn't know what it was.

Sunday had also reinforced his sense that a particular cloud threatened Tynie's Place. A knot of fear settled in his gut. He fought to replace it with determination.

He thought of Sylvia and didn't even try to separate his personal issues from his professional ones. It couldn't be done, would serve no purpose anyway.

In his mind he replayed the moment when he'd taken her in the shower. He'd lifted her, wrapping her around him. When he pushed inside her, he'd nearly fallen to his knees with the feeling of being home, of belonging. He held her, rocking, simply being one with her until she lifted her head from his shoulder to look at him with questions in her eyes. Their gazes held as he began to move inside her. Without words, he tried to make her see the answers.

No separation. The gangs threatened Sylvia, they threatened him. He would find a way to stop it.

It was nearly dusk—though no later than five. Marisel and Sylvia sat at the kitchen table, talking over tea. Their patient, Kiesha, was asleep upstairs. Her labor was a long, slow one, exhausting her. They'd given her a shot of narcotics to let her rest. They sent most of her family home for the same purpose. Only the baby's father had stayed, napping now with her in the big double bed of the birth room.

The two women were talking about gangs.

"You know I won't close this place."

"Bah, Sylvie. Things are going to get worse. Maybe we won't keep our girls safe here. What happens then?"

"If we close, then what happens is that the gangs win. No one stands for the community, for the women and children who live here."

"Honey, you're a strong woman. You can control a lot of things in your life. But I don't know if you can control this."

"The women should be on our side—the girlfriends, the mothers. It's their men who are going to die and they know it."

"But what can they do? You know how our girls are—they're afraid to say no to the boys. They're afraid to lose them."

"The girls are into the gangs, too."

Sylvia and Marisel looked to the kitchen door, surprised. It was Terry, the young father-to-be. He rubbed his face, still looking sleepy as he walked over to the coffeepot. "They get status if their man is important in the gang. They get money, bling. Many girls will put up with a lot for that. They won't want to change it. They don't get those things if their man works at McDonalds."

Sylvia motioned for him to bring his coffee and join them at the table. He'd just spoken a painful truth, one Sylvia could not deny. "Okay. The gangs provide a social structure in a community that lacks them, and a source of income and self-respect. I'll accept I can't change that. But I can't accept young men getting shot on my doorstep. I need to keep Tynie's Place safe."

"You need sanctuary."

Sylvie considered, then nodded. The term traditionally applied to churches in settings of strife. But it was essentially what she wanted. "Yes."

"Can you buy it?"

"What? Pay money to the gangs to make this a safe place?"

"It might be the simplest way."

She thought about it, wondered how much it would take, wondered if she could stomach the thought of buying protection from organizations perpetrating violence and abuse.

"What else? Give me another way."

The young man shrugged. He and Kiesha had only been with the birth center for a few weeks, but she liked the young couple. Terry was gentle and intelligent—he always treated Kiesha kindly and with respect. Sylvia knew he took courses at the community college.

She waited, but he said no more. "There must be something."

"What do you have that they want?"

Sylvia and Marisel eyed each other. Slowly they smiled. Marisel spoke first. "We could tell all the girls that they have infections. We could say they can't have sex."

"I do the baby boys' circumcisions. I could tell them how I have to be very careful not to cut too much. That if I get nervous I might make a mistake."

They both giggled, though Terry didn't seem to see the humor. "We could let it slip that there could be some question about a particular baby's paternity."

"We could do an exam and then tell the girls they got warts from their partners."

Terry finally cracked a smile. "Ouch. You women are mean."

They all laughed for a moment, then sobered, looking at each other, searching for an answer. No easy ones came. After a while, Sylvia let the subject go. "What are you studying at MCC, Terry?"

"Mostly biology. I was good at it in high school."

"Good for you. I know a biology professor at U of R. He's kind of a cantankerous old guy, not easy to please. But he could tell you if you have what it takes to study there. You know about the two plus two program, don't you, for MCC students transferring to U of R?"

"Yes, I know. I've thought about it—but a lot of students fail."

"This guy could help you figure out if it would work for you. It wouldn't hurt to talk with him—much."

She smiled as he took the challenge. "Okay. I'd like that."

She started to say she would give the professor a call, but the sight of a man standing in the doorway took her breath. It was Emilio, but panic threatened in the few seconds before she recognized him.

He looked like a soldier armed for battle. He was dressed in dark fatigues and carried a duffle that would handily accommodate a small arsenal. He nodded to Sylvia, then to Marisel—eyes lingering there, a bit, Sylvia thought. But when he spoke, it was directed at Terry. "Nephew."

Terry stood. "Uncle."

"What are you doing here?"

"Kiesha's in labor."

"I didn't know she was coming here."

"We transferred from the hospital clinic a few weeks ago."

"How is she doing?"

"Things are going kind of slow. She's sleeping now."

Emilio nodded but remained silent. Terry looked around at the three older people, taking in the tension. "I think I'll go check on her." He looked to Sylvia for approval and then left the room, skirting around Emilio's imposing form.

Emilio watched the young man leave, then turned back to the women.

Sylvia lifted her brow in curiosity. "'Uncle?'"

Emilio nodded. "He was my nephew's best friend—they'd been buddies since kindergarten, when Terry stood up to a third grade bully for my nephew. When his mother OD'd, my sister took him in. He still lives with her. He calls her 'mom.' That makes me 'uncle.'"

Sylvia smiled, impressed as always at the ease with which love and loyalty could overcome racial boundaries. Then she sobered and crossed her arms over her chest. "You didn't know Kiesha was in labor. So why are you here?"

"I plan to sleep here tonight. One of us—Coop or I—will be here every night until things quiet down some."

Sylvia opened her mouth, ready to object, but he stopped her with a raised hand. "We're not negotiating this."

"We will not contribute to the violence."

"You know that's not what this is about. You know we just want to make sure that you're safe." With a look, he included Marisel, who stood now with her arm around Sylvia. "We'll keep your patients safe, too."

Sylvia bit down on her temper. That last was a low blow. She might object to men walking into her life and taking control, but she could hardly argue with a measure that would protect those she cared for. Still—"And what patients would those be? No one will come for care in a building occupied by the police."

"We're here for personal reasons, to protect our women." Sylvia felt Marisel's breath catch, felt her stand straighter as the man declared for her with his eyes. "They will understand that."

Sylvia looked to the duffle bag. Some things she could not accept. "No guns."

"Not negotiable."

She huffed out a breath and started to turn away, but Marisel held her. "Honey."

Sylvie stubbornly looked at the floor, refusing to lift her head.

"Cooper loves you. You know what kind of man he is. Can you expect him to see danger around you and do nothing? Do you accept the man or not?"

Sylvia held back a frustrated moan. That was the question, indeed. Her friend was right: Cooper was a warrior. Accepting him would mean accepting the consequences of that, too. She raised her head to look at Marisel, then Emilio. Who was also, it appeared, a warrior at heart.

She lifted her hands, let them drop, relenting at least for the moment. She turned to walk past Emilio, meeting his eyes, knowing that her frustration showed. He watched her calmly, perhaps with some sympathy.

Before she reached the door, he spoke. "I locked the front door. From now on, after dark, it gets locked, stays locked."

She was going to object. Laboring patients and their families came and went all hours of the night. But she saw the answer in his face. Not negotiable.

She sighed and glanced back at Marisel. "I'll be in the gym."

She walked out of the kitchen, knowing the two she left behind now had eyes only for each other. The pleasure of that lightened her heart some.

Emilio watched Marisel, looking for some response to the claim he'd just made on her. She wouldn't meet his gaze. Instead she busied herself clearing dishes. Inwardly, he groaned. He was way out of touch with the modern courtship dance. When he'd married, young and in Puerto Rico, it had been arranged by his parents and hers. He'd barely known the girl before their wedding night.

He rubbed the back of his neck. "The gym?"

"We have a play room for the day care. Sylvie put some exercise equipment in it, hoping that the girls would use it, you know, become more physically active. Sylvie uses it on long call shifts, when she can't leave the center. Sometimes she works out her troubles there."

"I guess Cooper and I are part of her troubles now. I'm sorry for it."

Marisel nodded. "Sí. Though perhaps you are part of the solution, too, eh? I think maybe your friend can make her happy."

"I hope so."

"It will not always be easy for her. She is independent, has been too much on her own. A strong man like Cooper is right for her. But he scares her. It's life, you know? To get something, you have to give something up. She's afraid to give up too much of herself to him."

He moved in closer, came up behind her where she worked at the sink. He put his hands on the counter, on either side of her, closing her in. Her hands slipped on the dish she rinsed. He liked the way she moved, leaning back a little towards him. He could see her reflection in the window over the sink, and their eyes met there.

"How about you, Mari? Are you willing to give yourself to a man?"

"It's been a long time, many years."

"And for me."

"You were married?"

"I was, when I was very young. She had a problem with her pregnancy. She died, the baby with her."

"I'm sorry."

"It was long ago. What about you, Mari?"

"I gave myself to a boy, and he gave me Lilibeth. He would not marry me."

"You have regrets, then?"

"No. I'm glad to have my daughter, and my grandbaby now. Also—there was fire, passion between us. That is part of life, too, eh?"

"I think maybe we can still have passion, have fire, don't

you?"

"Emilio, in just a few years I will be forty."

He smiled. "And you have this spot, just here, beneath your ear that I have wanted to put my lips to since the first night I saw you."

He went in close, so she could feel his breath. She tilted her head just a little, giving him room. As he'd wanted, he put his lips against her. For a moment he didn't move, just breathed in her scent. Then he began to explore, kissing, tasting. Only his mouth touched her, but still he held her surrounded with his body.

After a while her breath caught. She leaned her head onto his shoulder and reached up to put her hand against his cheek. He turned his head a little to kiss her palm.

"Mari." He put his hands at her waist, stroked his thumbs along her ribs. "I want to check the building—see that doors and windows are secure. Can I come to you later?"

"I'll be in my apartment—in the back, up on the second floor. Unless Kiesha gets active, then I'll be with her and Terry."

"Where are Lilibeth and your grandchild?"

"They're away. A friend of Lilibeth's just had a baby. She's still in the hospital. Lilibeth is at her house, taking care of her two little children."

"Then I can come to you?"

"*Si*, Emilio."

As dark fell, Cooper stood on a small side street just off Thurston. A cold rain drizzled, a few flakes of snow mixed in. For the first hour he was there, activity on the street had lessened. He made no effort to hide who he was or what he was doing. He just stood leaning against a lamppost, watching.

Young men warmed themselves around a barrel fire, talking loudly, heads bobbing to hip hop, and watched him back. Cars slowly passed along the block, drivers no doubt frustrated when no one approached their window, small packages ready to barter for the cash they brought with them.

Finally, one brash young man sauntered up to a car window. He kept his eyes on Cooper as the exchange was made. When Cooper made no move, the man strutted back to his buddies and the car drove off. Gradually, business picked up. Cooper watched.

Emilio found Marisel's door left open a bit. The rest of the building was quiet—activity only in the gym where Sylvia ran at an impressive pace on a treadmill, Donna Summer blasting out a rapid beat, and quiet whispers in the dark behind the closed door of one of the birth rooms.

He stood at the door, pushed it quietly open until he saw her. She sat in a rocking chair, knitting something small, something for babies, he guessed. The needles clicked away, but he heard them stutter when she became aware of him. She continued with them for another minute then they gradually stilled. She looked up at him, the quiet now palpable.

She gave no signal that he could read. He accepted that at least there was no objection, and after a few moments he closed the door behind him and walked to her. He knelt beside her chair, breathed in her scent. He put his hands over hers, stripping away the needles and yarn. Carefully— enough, he hoped—he set the lot of it in the basket on the floor.

"I think, when I kiss a woman for the first time, it's better if she does not have sharp, pointy objects in her hands."

She smiled, but there was a bit of a tremor in it. He was pretty sure it was nervousness, not excitement. To his endless relief, she reached up to stroke his face. Watching her eyes, he grasped her hand, held it to him, then began to make love to it with his mouth. When his tongue stroked her palm, she shuddered.

"*Dios mio.*"

"*Si*, Mari." He held her hand against his cheek. Touching her nowhere else, he leaned forward until his lips hovered over hers. "Do you give yourself to me, *querida*?"

Her mouth moved, forming the word, *si*, but only a whisper of breath came out. He watched that mouth, enticed by lush, ruby lips and a hint of pink tongue beyond.

He put his free hand along her neck, felt the rising beat of her pulse. Slowly he lowered his head, fitted his lips to hers. He rubbed and stroked, then sank into the sweet heat of her.

A few minutes later he stood. He lifted her and carried her to bed.

Kiesha labored through the night, finally giving birth in the wee hours of the morning to little Serene', round-cheeked and capped with long black curls. Sylvia helped the couple through most of the labor. When Marisel joined them to assist with the birth, Sylvia gave her enough of a perusal to have a blush rising on the older woman's face. Marisel answered her grin with a sharp look that had Sylvie chuckling.

They tucked the young couple and their baby in for a nap with the plan that Marisel would pack them off to home in a few hours. Sylvia finished up the paperwork, then bundled into her coat. It was light outside, after nine.

She walked through the birth center, satisfied with her night's work, more than happy that another midwife would cover her office visits for the day.

As she passed the family waiting room, she stopped to extend her congratulations. Emilio had his arm around his sister, Hildie. Sylvia had seen how close she and Terry were; the new honorary grandmother made no effort to hide the tears as she held little Serene' for the first time.

When Marisel joined the group, Emilio brought her to his side. He kept her there with a hand at her waist as he introduced her to his sister. Hildie's eyes lit as she observed her brother's behavior, then with a wide smile she wrapped Marisel in her arms.

Emilio caught sight of Sylvia and pulled her into the room with a hug that lifted her off her feet. He planted a noisy kiss on her cheek. "You do good work, little sister."

"Kiesha and Terry did the hard part."

"And a fine job they did of it, too, eh?"

She laughed at his exuberance. "Yes."

Sylvia left the three of them, Marisel and Hildie huddled together on the couch, Emilio looking a bit bemused.

She stepped outside, took in the red GTO across the street, and the big handsome hunk leaning against it. Leather jacket, snug blue jeans, and a day's beard could surely look good on a man.

Smiling, she crossed to him, aware of his attention on her. He didn't move except to lower his head a little when she lifted up to touch lips. She liked leaning into him while he had his arms still crossed over his chest, liked his strength, his scent.

"Emilio's an uncle again."

"Yeah, I saw him strutting. You'd think he was the one who made it all happen. More." He nudged at her for her lips until she made a proper kiss of it. He was starting to show a lot of interest, had moved a hand to grab at her jacket, when she pulled back.

"I need to sleep."

"Me, too. Your place or mine?"

She leaned back more and shot him a pointed look. "I mean, really sleep."

"I'm sure we'll get there." He nibbled at her. "I've got a hot tub." He pulled her back against him, bit gently at her lower lip. He hummed a little, and she felt the need rising between them. "Come on."

Opening the driver's side door, he nudged her in and then across the seat so he could climb in next to her. She leaned her head against his shoulder, breathing in the scent of leather. Bruce Springsteen filled the interior with words of hope, from a sound system much upgraded from the car's original AM/FM.

He watched the rearview mirror as he pulled away from the curb and started down the block. He turned the corner and passed the first house or two, then brought the car to a stop. He watched again in the mirror.

After a few moments, he paused the CD player. He picked up the ear set for his cell phone and punched in a preset. Then he spoke. "Hey, Brett. Cooper Billings. Run a plate for me, will you? You can text page me when you find it." He listed a license plate number and hung up with a brief thanks.

"What was that about?"

Cooper set the phone aside, held her gaze for a few seconds, and then kissed her before looking back to the road.

"Maybe nothing. There was a car parked down the street when you came out of the birth center. I didn't see anybody get in or out, but he pulled away when we did." He put a hand on her thigh and squeezed gently. "Just being careful."

He parked outside his garage and took her in through the side door. She got only a glimpse of gardens well tucked for winter. "We're kind of under construction, here," he said, taking her past a kitchen that was wrecked. "But my bedroom is nearly done and the bathroom is great."

He led her up the stairs, and she was enchanted. He'd opened up the space, with half of the second story devoted to his bedroom. The room had expansive windows to the north for the view and to either side for morning and afternoon light. Varnished wood gleamed on the floor, matched by the window woodwork that was still in progress. French doors opened to a small balcony that faced the city and lake, where two comfortable outdoor recliners and a telescope were situated.

Inside, the walls were painted a cool green, warmed by turquoise and cherry red bedding and accents. The raised bed was bleached wood and very large.

He smiled as her gaze settled on it. He leaned down to kiss her cheek. "Make yourself comfortable. Help yourself to anything you want. There's a robe in the closet, tee shirts in the second drawer over there. I'm going to start the tub."

He kept his eyes on her as he removed his jacket and dropped it on a chair. He kissed her again before he walked to the bathroom. There was more space there, she could see, and light drizzling through the skylights and glass block wall. A large hot tub and a separate, complicated and luxurious shower cubicle were visible.

Sylvia sighed, unable to deny how good, how right it felt to be with Cooper. He was like no man she'd been attracted to before. He was a powerful force, strong not just physically but in determination and will. He had no compunction about going after what he wanted.

Now he wanted her. It was unsettling but, she had to admit, also exciting and gratifying. His desire for her was seductive; it would be easy to slide into it, be overtaken by it.

He would share his strength with her, generously, and he would think to protect her. He wouldn't consider that to do so would threaten her own strength. He wouldn't easily see that

his power could overwhelm her and that she could lose herself.

She fingered her coat—she'd been about to take it off.
Now she wondered if she'd be smarter to turn and run from
this room. She even looked for a moment toward the door.

Then she felt his eyes on her, and she turned back to
face him. His shirt was gone, his jeans unfastened. Muscles
rippled across his chest and bulged in the arm he had leaned
up against the doorway of the bathroom. She could see the
dark tuft of hair under his arm, and she knew his scent would
be there.

He watched her as if aware that she was considering
bolting. Despite his strength there was a vulnerability in him,
an uncertainty that quieted her worries.

She slipped out of her coat. She knew the gleam in his
eyes that came then should make her wary. But it heated,
hungered, as she unbuttoned her shirt, and she felt a little
riff of pleasure at her own power.

She wanted him, too. There was strength in that as well.

Anyway, she wasn't going to love him. He was a cop.

They were quietly lazy in the tub, letting the heat work
on their fatigue, sinking into it. He held her against him,
touching and stroking just enough to keep a little sexual
edge.

He'd been able to read her easily. He didn't know if it was
a blessing or a curse. She'd been close to running, and he
wasn't sure if it had been anything more than plain and simple lust that had kept her.

She was a sensual woman who gave herself over to the
physical pleasures of sex. He was immensely grateful for
that.

He wanted more.

She was nearly asleep when he lifted her from the tub,
handing her a warm towel to wrap herself in. He led her to
the bed and turned it down. Facing her, close enough so
their bodies touched, he reached between them and closed
his fist over the knot that held the towel at her breasts.

He tugged, chafing the soft terry cloth down over her,

watching as the tops of her breasts and then her nipples were released. Her breath caught and her nipples, soft and glowing from the heat of the bath, tightened as he watched.

Sylvia swayed a little, and he turned his fist to tighten the towel at her waist, steadying her. He kept his eyes on her breasts, enjoying both the view and the way his gaze on her seemed to shake her.

She trembled when he lifted his free hand and ran his finger over the very tip of her nipple. He rubbed back and forth with greater pressure until he caught at it with his thumb and finger. She cried out as he squeezed.

He held her there by her nipple and with his other hand moved the towel lower. When he reached her thighs he pushed into her, inserting cloth and fist between her legs. He pressed up against her, urging.

She complied, rubbing herself against the towel and his fist. She gripped at his arms, dropped her head back with a moan. He leaned over her, running tongue and teeth over her exposed neck.

The towel became an annoyance, a barrier between him and her heat. He dropped it, pushing it to the floor. Then his fingers took her, pressing into her wetness.

He stroked her hard until she convulsed, clenching about his fingers. Before it was over he pushed her back so she lay across his bed, her legs dangling. Placing his hands on her thighs he lifted them, opened them, then put his tongue on her. In her.

She came again with a cry, bucking and clutching at his hair. He rose over her, an arm under her waist sliding her to the center of the bed. He put his mouth on hers, his tongue delving, then plunged his shaft into her.

Connected, made one, they found an eye in the storm that had taken them. His body stilled and he lifted his head. Gently, he ran his fingers over her face until she opened her eyes to him.

While they watched each other, he stroked inside her once, hard. She arched up against him, seeking. Their fingers entwined, grasping and holding tight.

His body taut, he held himself over her. Tension spiraled. Their breath came in ragged pants as they strained against each other. Still, he held her where they joined, where he speared into her.

Then the eye passed. Some movement of hers sent a shock of pleasure through him, and the storm raged again. He drove into her, pounding. She flexed her hips, answering each thrust. Fingers ran over heated skin, grasping, leaving marks.

He tugged where his fingers tangled in her hair, pulling her head back and arching her breasts up to be ravished by his mouth. He clutched her in his arms, plunging, in and out, until a brutal climax took them both. He emptied into her in hot spasms.

She shuddered in little aftershocks when he pulled out of her. He rolled to his side next to her, pulled the covers up to tuck in around them both, and snugged her tight with an arm at her waist. "Sleep. Now sleep."

She was already gone. He nestled her head against his shoulder, felt with his thumb the tear on her cheek.

There was still some light when she woke, but it came from the windows to the west and was nearly gone. She turned her head toward the warmth and found she was wrapped in Cooper's arms. His head was propped on pillows; he watched her wake.

It was a lovely feeling, waking warm and secure, watched over. She stretched a little in pleasure, feeling indulged. "Are you working nights tonight? Or back to days?"

"Days. I'll sleep again tonight. How about you?"

"Me, too. I have a midwife covering for me today and to-night. I won't work again until tomorrow."

"Have you had enough sleep, then?"

"Um-hmm. I feel great." She met his eyes. "You know how to put a woman to sleep."

He lifted his brow a little. "And that's a good thing?"

She smiled. "In my job it is."

He softly touched her lips with his. "My pleasure. Anytime. I'd be glad to be on call for the task."

She chuckled, then pushed him over so she could rest against him with her head on his shoulder. She breathed in and out, knowing his scent was a part of her now. Her fingers tangled in the silver chain around his neck. She rubbed her thumb over the cross that lay on his chest.

"You gave this to me the night I was hurt."

"Um-hmm."

"To keep me safe?"

"Mmm."

"Tell me."

He pressed his hand over hers, securing it over his chest. Her palm covered the cross. She felt the strong thud of his heartbeat.

"My partner in Baltimore gave it to me. Teddy Washington. His old Baptist grandmother gave it to him when he went on the job. Said it would protect him."

He was quiet for a while, stoking her hand. "It did, until one night we were out on a drug bust. We were after a new heroin connection. The force had staked out the harbor for weeks. We were close to the top players."

She waited through another pause.

"We expected to pick up the number two guy that night. He was there to oversee the transfer at the port. They were ready for us. We had twenty guys there that night. Two died. We had three injured. One was Teddy."

He twined his fingers with hers, enclosing the cross. "He went out on disability. He works security now. He gave the cross to me, said I'd need it more."

Her hand on his chest rose and fell with his breath. She knew there was more.

"We never got the guy. We were so close. I could feel him."

"You left." She was surprised. He wasn't the sort to abandon a battle midway through it. And he'd have wanted to avenge his partner.

"Yeah." He lifted his head to look at her. "I had a fiancée at the time."

She arched her eyebrows. "Do tell."

He dropped his head back, gazed at the ceiling. He lifted a hand to trail fingers through her hair. "That night kind of ended it for us."

"She was afraid for you."

"No. She was pissed I spent the night with Teddy at the hospital. It was her parents' anniversary. I was supposed to be at the country club for the big party."

"She was afraid for you, too."

"She was embarrassed. She wanted me off the job. She wanted me to work in a nice, big corporate office. Wear a suit." He took her fingers, still holding the cross, to his lips.

"She didn't have much heart, Sylvie."

"She loved you."

He shook his head. "Not that much. She wasn't happy with me. My parents, also of the country club set, weren't happy with me. When Laurie and I broke up, I figured it was better to leave."

"What made you choose Rochester?"

She felt his lips curve in a smile. "Apparently, there was a woman waiting for me here. One with a lot of heart, but in need of rescue."

She smiled, too, remembering how he'd taken her into his arms on the night they'd met. "And..."

"Travis Sullivan recruited me. He was interested in the strategy the Baltimore force had implemented for gang and street crime."

Sylvia stifled a laugh. She'd have to have a word with Travis Sullivan.

He lifted his head again, brought her close, kissed her thoroughly. "Remind me to thank him again."

She pulled back enough to look at him before he got too interested. "I want you to tell me about gangs."

He dropped his head back and sighed. "As pillow talk, the part about how well I put you to sleep was a lot better."

"I need to know."

"You can't fight them yourself."

"I have to understand them better, Coop. I have to figure out how to keep Tynie's Place safe."

He was quiet for so long she thought he might not talk to her. Then he sighed again. "Well, we can't have this conversation on empty stomachs. How about a pizza?"

"Are you talking in bed, or do we have to dress and go out?"

"You eat pizza in bed?" He shook his head, tut-tutting in apparent distaste. "Where have you been all my life?"

They lounged against pillows, a box with pepperoni and onions between them. He wore only his jeans, button open at the waist, and the rosy glow of sunset on his chest and shoulders. As tempting to taste as the pizza, he quite distracted her.

She wore her skimpy panties and one of his tee shirts knotted above. He liked the look of both of them on her; he'd told her so in words and with his eyes. He looked a bit distracted, too. She was not above taking pleasure in that. Every once in awhile, just to keep his interest, she ran the toes of her left foot up her right calf, resting them at her knee. The heat in his eyes as they followed that movement, centering where her open thighs joined, was superbly gratifying.

This time he stopped in mid-sentence. "You do that again and you're going to find yourself flat on your back, with me inside you."

Living dangerously, she smiled and waggled her knee a little.

He reached for the pizza box, ready to send it flying. "Do you think I'm not serious?"

She laughed and straightened up against the pillows. "Okay. I'll be good. Keep talking."

He watched her a minute while he took a long pull from his beer bottle, letting her see his indecision. Finally he settled back into the bed and picked up his thread.

"We've had gangs here in the city for years—loose groups of mostly young kids, say, fifteen to twenty years old. Groups like the Thurston Zoo, the Dipset. Not much structure, no hierarchy. Their actions have been largely disorganized, often spontaneous. That's been true even for the two largest gangs—the Plymouth Rocks and the Latin Kings.

"In the last few weeks it looks like there's been a change, at least in the Rocks. They've been acting more like big city gangs: hazing rituals for new members, a council that regulates gang actions, discipline within the group that includes punishment for rogue activity. Punishment that may include death."

He watched for a moment, making sure, she knew, that she understood the warning in that. "Gangs want power, territory, money. Well-organized gangs have a plan to get those things. A business plan, if you will. In those circumstances gang behavior becomes more focused than random.

"Gangs like the Cribs have franchises in some cities. That may be what we're seeing here—an imported boss. Or it might be a dominant leader has emerged locally, someone smart, charismatic, and power-hungry."

He stopped and swigged again at his beer while he pondered. He watched her, but she knew he was tugging at some internal thread. She waited quietly until his attention focused on her, still considering.

"The car I saw this morning is registered to Noah Parsons."

That sent a chill down her spine. Then she caught his drift. "And he's someone who's smart, charismatic, and power-hungry? That's a stretch, isn't it, Coop? A city councilman as gang kingpin?"

"Why was he out there, Sylvie?"

She shook her head, asking herself the same question. She didn't like any answer that came to mind. "He might have been watching you, not me."

"He wants you. He'd want you anyway, but he particularly wants you in order to spite me. It's a sure bet he didn't like watching you come to me this morning."

She'd walked right up to him and kissed him, driven away with him. "What does he have against you?"

Cooper shrugged. "I knew him in law school. Back then he threw money around—slick clothes, pricey cars, flashy women. I didn't know his background then. Now I do. I think he threw more money around than his family had to give him. Now I have to wonder where he got it.

"Anyway, this 'man of the 'hood' thing he's got going is an act. I know it. He knows I know it. He doesn't mind flaunting it."

"He doesn't seem to see you as a threat. He's wrong, isn't he?"

He smiled grimly. "Oh, yeah." Then he took her hand, brought it to his mouth. "He knows my weakness, though. I need you to be careful."

A twinge of guilt nudged at her. She squeezed his hand, hoping he'd take that as reassurance. Then she pulled back. "So gangs make money through drugs."

He nodded, watching her. "And prostitution in some cities, though we haven't seen that here, yet."

"Is the drug trade getting more organized here?"

He nodded again, approving of her logic. "Maybe. Heroin's making a significant comeback. We've had a few OD's in emergency—it looks like the gangs have it. We're trying to trace the source."

She lay back on the bed, watching the light move over the ceiling as the sun set. The last sliver was gone before she spoke again. "Terry thought I might be able to buy protection."

"No."

"No? Because they wouldn't honor it?"

"No, because to do that you'd have to negotiate with them, and you're not going to negotiate with gangs."

She looked at him, hearing the hard edge in his voice. "Because...?"

"Jesus." This time he did take the pizza box and fling it off the end of the bed. He moved to cover her, gripping her jaw, his face in hers. He searched her eyes. "Because it's not safe. Because I could never let you. Because I couldn't live with it if you were hurt again."

She took some steadying breaths, trying to calm the pulse that had leaped within her. "Tynie's Place is mine, Cooper. I built it. It's my job to protect it."

"No, Sylvie. It's your job to deliver babies, goddammit. Emilio and I will be there. The whole force is working on the gang problem. That's *our* job." His fingers held like clamps on her face. "Promise me you won't approach them."

She met his eyes but didn't speak.

He waited, becoming visibly more incensed. When he realized he wouldn't get her promise, he jerked away from her. He rose and strode from the bed, slapping his hand against the wall, cursing creatively. Then he leaned before a window, hands raised on the frame, head hanging.

She rose to her knees, forced herself to keep from reaching out to him.

Finally he raised his head and turned, hands planted on his hips, looking every bit the warrior. His eyes were fierce, battle-ready. "You won't accept me because I'm a cop. You say you can't live with the thought that I could get hurt or killed on the job. It's what I do. I'm good at it, and I'm careful. I'm trained. I carry a gun, for God's sake. I'm a—"

She lifted her brow, waiting for him to finish that sentence. When he didn't, she did. "A man?"

"Yes, dammit, and I don't apologize for it. It's not sexist that men protect the women and children; it's biology."

"What about women cops?"

He pulled at his hair. "This is not about women on the job. It's about you and me. It's about wanting you safe enough that I can sleep at night."

"You're allowed that? But I'm not?"

"It's different."

"I don't see how."

He walked to the bed, leaned down in front of her. "Sylvie. One of us has been shot while at work. It was the midwife, not the cop."

She pushed to her feet, putting the bed between them. "You don't own me, Cooper. I may sleep with you but I don't— You're not my—"

His eyes blazed, challenging her to finish. When she didn't, he turned away. He picked up his shirt from the floor and grabbed his jacket. "Get dressed, please. I'll take you home." He went through the door without turning back.

He drove in silence. Sylvie sat beside him, huddled into her jacket. It didn't help. The cold came from within. She cursed herself for allowing his rejection to hurt so much, for letting her feelings for him get so far out of control.

When he pulled up in front of her house, he left the car running. She reached for the door handle without looking at him. He stayed her with a hand on her arm. He got out, circled the car, and opened the door for her.

He walked behind her to the steps, stood as she unlocked her door. She was through the door, behind the screen before she looked up at him.

His eyes compelled her to pause in the act of closing the door. He put his hand to the screen. He spoke quietly. "You love me, Sylvie. Even if you're not ready to know it, you do. If you didn't, you'd never give yourself to me as you do."

He stopped, his gaze seeming to search her soul. "We're going to find a way to work this out. We have to."

He waited, and she knew what he wanted. Unable to do otherwise, she lifted her hand, pressed palm and fingers to his through the screen. After a long moment, he spoke.

"Lock up." Then he was gone.

CHAPTER NINE

The mayor of Rochester was unhappy with all the dead bodies on his streets. When he was unhappy, everyone under his power felt it. The chief of police felt it, and he didn't stint either when it came to sharing the pain.

Complicated strategies developed by academics were out. Immediate, visible action was in.

Rochester City Police spent the week picking up gang members. A total of seventeen boys and men were arrested. The charges related to robbery, controlled substances, assault, and murder. Any violations that involved illegal guns were transferred to federal court. The district attorney's office, in an unprecedented agreement with the Police Department, announced they would offer reduced sentences or plea bargains only to defendants who gave effective information against other gang members.

The goal was to break the gangs by sentencing as many of them as possible to long prison terms. It was a limited solution; certain members of the community were opposed, concerned about the long-term effects on young men's lives. But it was something the police department could do, and they did it that week with a vengeance.

Cooper and Emilio knew the players as well as anyone. They were actively involved or behind the scenes in many of the arrests. The action kept Cooper busy. Not enough to keep him from thinking about Sylvia, but enough to keep him from doing anything about her.

He was grateful the job kept him in check. The desire to have her in his arms was strong, enough to override his better sense. Only exhaustion let him sleep at night; many times he came close to going to her.

He needed some time. He'd taken her home so abruptly on Monday night because he was afraid of what he might do. Her refusal to reassure him that she wouldn't try to approach the gangs on her own was like a slap in the face.

He accepted that it was primitive, this drive to protect her, keep her safe. Her willingness to thwart it raised the beast in him.

He knew it wasn't wrong, the force in him that compelled him to guard her. He was a man; it was his job. It was in his nature.

He understood she was a strong woman. That was part of what he loved about her. It had come as a surprise, something new to him. He'd never before thought about a woman's strength, valued what a woman could accomplish through grit and determination.

Now he had to figure out how to live with it. He was pretty sure the urge that burned in him to lock her away, safe forever in his bedroom, wasn't the right approach. He couldn't break her, wouldn't want to.

She was going to have to learn how to bend.

Worse, so was he.

So he'd take some time to make his own adjustments, time to find a strategy to apply to her. Long days and nights on the job were a good thing.

Besides, it was game week.

On Friday morning, Sylvia and Marisel drank tea at the kitchen table. The night had been quiet—they'd had only one other birth since Kiesha and Terry's baby. Though the birth center had been empty, each night that week either Cooper or Emilio had slept there.

Sylvia was aware of the nights when Emilio was there—Marisel tended to sleep late, and Emilio would shyly tiptoe out of her rooms in the morning.

She never saw Cooper. The first night he came late and Marisel set him to sleep in the smaller of the birth rooms. He was gone early in the morning, before Sylvia arrived. Another morning, she came in early and heard him showering, but he was out the door and gone again without stopping by the kitchen where she'd put coffee on.

She did a poor job convincing herself she was glad he'd made himself scarce. Yet she knew it was for the best. Already, she missed him, had the feeling that life wasn't right without him. The more they saw each other, the harder it would be to let him go, as she knew she must.

It was a relief, really, to have him be the one to pull back. It was easier to accept his rejection than to constantly wonder if she was simply a coward, refusing to fall in love with him. Or, worse, if she could still claim not to love him.

Easier, but not easy. She was frustrated and unhappy. And the well-pleasured glow that suffused Marisel's face was totally annoying.

"I guess you had a good night."

Marisel nearly stifled her sigh. All in all, she'd been fairly indulgent of Sylvia's bad mood. Apparently whatever happened in her bedroom at night made her tolerant.

"It's good to have a good man. You could have one, too. Why don't you?"

"I told you, he took me home." After incredibly hot and loving sex. "He left and he hasn't come back. Hasn't called." Had made significant effort to avoid her, in fact.

"Bah. You have him wrapped around your finger. Emilio says he's as grumpy as you are. All you have to do is go to him."

"I don't want to go to him. I'm not dying to have a man. I just wish you would stop looking so damned satisfied."

"*Si*. I can try to do that."

The smirk on Marisel's face finally cracked Sylvie's bad humor. "Oh, just tell me to shut up."

"It's okay. Cooper's not going to be able to take much more of this. He'll come jump you, and then you will look satisfied, too."

"You know it's not going to work out, Mari."

"*Si*. What you say."

Sylvia muttered, "*Si*," under her breath and stood to clear the table. "What does our schedule look like today?"

"Just the morning—five or six prenatal visits."

"Good. I'm going to go see Danniqwa and Alejandro this afternoon. He's just got out of the hospital."

"You want me to go, do her postpartum visit?"

"No, thanks. I want to see them."

Danniqwa sniffed back her tears as she watched Alejandro cuddle Aniya in his arms. He sat in a wheelchair, but assured Sylvia that, with physical therapy, he was walking better every day. A guitar sat propped in a corner. His upper body strength was good; he could still play.

Sylvia spent a few minutes enjoying the young couple's enchantment with their daughter. They nuzzled and teased until they got a smile, and bragged about the two pounds she'd gained already. Danniqwa avidly soaked up advice on breastfeeding and sleep habits.

When she offered something to drink, Sylvia asked for hot tea.

Alone with Alejandro and the baby, she knelt beside the wheelchair. Resting her palms on her thighs, she looked at the young, wounded man. "Alejandro, I need to meet with the Latin Kings."

He shot her a sharp glance, then looked back to Aniya. Not speaking, he shook his head.

"Please. You know why I'm asking. I have to protect Tynie's Place."

He turned to her abruptly, anger blazing in his eyes. "You don't know what you're asking."

The baby startled and Alejandro turned back to her, soothing her against his chest.

Sylvia sat back, disturbed by that sudden flash of anger. So easily, he could have been one of them, the ungrounded young men who made the streets so mean.

She put a hand on his arm. "I'm sorry, Alejandro. I'll find another way."

"Another way to meet with the Kings?"

"Yes."

Brow furrowed, he looked at her, disapproval clear. Finally he spoke. "All right. My cousin Pedro works at the Sonic Car Wash on Lyell. I'll call and let you know when he'll be there."

"Thank you."

He shook his head. "Thank me later, if you come out of this alive and unharmed."

The car wash had seen better days, maybe before I 490 construction had taken so much traffic off city streets. The lot that once might have been filled with cars in line for a wash now sported several junkers with sale prices painted on their windshields. *Hope springs eternal*, Sylvia thought.

The young man behind the counter watched her approach. She knew he would be Pedro even before she saw the name on his stained overalls.

He looked her over. "You the midwife."

"Yes. My name's Sylvia Huston."

"You come to find out if I plugged Antwan Taylor?"

"No. Did you?"

"Mighta. If somebody else hadn't done him first."

"One of your pals beat you to it?"

"Nope. Not one of my pals."

Sylvia pondered that. "You mean, no one in the Kings?" He stayed quiet, watching her. "Who, then?"

"Somebody else don't like Antwan, I guess." He shrugged. "Don't matter. He got what he deserved."

"For hurting Alejandro?"

Another shrug. "He's family. Even if he pretends he ain't." He took some time lighting a cigarette. "He asked me to meet with you. He never asked me for anything before."

Sylvia felt the burden of that, aware of what the request had cost Alejandro, what it might cost him yet. "I delivered his baby. I helped him the night he was shot. He called you as a favor to me. I don't want him to come to grief over it."

Another lift of the shoulder. "Maybe someday he can do something for me. So what do you want?"

"I want to meet with the Kings. I want to ask for sanctuary for Tynie's Place."

He raised his eyebrows. "You think that will work?"

"How many of the babies born at Tynie's Place do you know? Alejandro's daughter. Your brother Ramos had two babies born there. How many others? Your friends? I know some Perez girls. Where do your sisters go for prenatal care or for birth control? How about your girlfriend?"

He ground out his cigarette on the scarred counter, belligerent eyes challenging her.

She drew a breath, reining in her temper. "If a member of the Kings is having a baby, he's welcome at Tynie's Place. I want to make sure he and his woman and baby are safe there."

"You want the Rocks to be safe, too."

"Yes. I'm going to ask the same of them."

"You got *cojones*, lady."

"Will you help?"

"Maybe I can get some guys together tonight. I'll call you."

"Thank you."

"Alejandro asked me to keep you safe. He asks a lot."

"Leave him alone."

"You ask a lot, too."

Late that night, Sylvia walked alone into an abandoned building. She'd noted with irony that it used to be a medical office. Just inside the door, Pedro met her and motioned her to follow.

The dark hall echoed with their footsteps. She tried to calm her galloping heartbeat, almost afraid she wouldn't be able to hear above it. She didn't know if she was doing the right thing, just that it was the only thing she knew to do.

She did know it was dangerous, maybe foolish. The image of Cooper stormed in her mind, incensed at her behavior. And rightfully so, she had to admit. She herself thought she must be crazy. She didn't need him in her head, telling her so.

She followed the dark jacket in front of her until they entered a back room. A flickering florescent light dangled from the ceiling, its buzz loud in the silence. A dozen Latin Kings lounged or sat on a banged-up arrangement of metal chairs, old desks, and even a scarred examination table. Their faces all turned to her, eyes gleaming out from under their jacket hoods, knit caps, and do-rags. No one smiled.

They were quiet as she looked back at them. When her eyes adjusted to the light and her nerves settled, she recognized some of them.

She nodded to one. "Edgardo. How's Marisa doing? She must have had a birthday by now. Is she walking yet?"

Edgardo looked back at her, not happy for her attention. Finally, he answered, a mumble. "She's fine. *Bueno.*"

She searched some more. "Ricky." On the street he was called Scoot, but she avoided using street names when young men came to the birth center. Ricky had been there three years ago, for the birth of his son. He'd proudly cut the cord. "I saw little Ricky at the drop-in last week, playing with a basketball. It looks like he has his daddy's hands."

Ricky gave one reluctant nod of his head.

She nodded at a couple of the others.

Finally one of them spoke. She'd seen him around, enough to know that everybody feared him. His name was

Jorge Rosario. "You wanted a meeting. It ain't a social. What you want, woman?"

She looked at him, spoke to him. "I want Tynie's Place to be safe. I can't keep it open if my patients can't come and go in safety. And I mean my patients, their babies, their babies' daddies, their families."

"Shit happen. It ain't always our business."

"I'm making it your business."

"How you doing that?"

"Starting in one week, if anything happens within three blocks of Tynie's Place, I close it. If girls are there for their appointments, I'll send them away. If someone is there in labor, I'll put her in an ambulance to the hospital. No groups. No day care. Nothing. I'll close for three days, anytime something happens."

"Define 'something.'"

"A robbery. A shooting. A boy's coat stolen. Somebody's *abuela* slips and falls on the ice. Anything I don't like."

"We don't control all that."

"You control a lot. I'm telling this to the Plymouth Rocks, too. As of next week, you'll just have to be sure nothing happens."

"What makes you think we care?"

"Oh, I don't think you care. But there are people in your lives who do. Aren't there?" She looked around again, making eye contact. "And if there aren't, then I'll be gone. I have no problem opening a nice, posh birth center out in the suburbs. No sweat."

"You want a three-block sanctuary around your place. What we get?"

"You know what you get. If you don't, talk to your women."

"I'd like to get the police off our backs."

"I have nothing to do with that."

"Sure you do. You doin' one of them." He smirked, looking around for appreciation of his cleverness.

"I don't control what he does in his work."

"Yeah, it looks like he don't control you too good, either. He know you're here, alone, pretty lady?" He stepped closer until he loomed over her.

She worked to keep her voice steady. "He's not a part of this."

"Make him a part of it. I'll deal with him, not you."
She shook her head. "Won't happen."
"Then we're done here." He put his hands on her hips, squeezed his fingers into her flesh. "Unless maybe you want to do a little more *negotiating*." He thrust his pelvis suggestively. "On your back."
She put a firm hand on his chest. She was aware of a little movement around her, Ricky and a couple others coming to their feet. She didn't know if they moved in support of her or presented more threat. Maybe Rosario didn't know either.
She pushed off from him, and he let her go. She backed away, then turned and walked out of the room.

As she did every November, Sylvia went with her mother to the firefighters-police football game. Though they had many friends among the RPD, they rooted for the firefighters. Sylvia's three O'Dade cousins played on that team. Katherine, formerly an O'Dade, had caused quite a stir when she married a cop; O'Dades had always fought fires.
It was a crisp, sunny fall day. The trees in Cobb's Hill Park were dropping the last of their leaves. Children played underneath, making a game of catching them before they hit the ground.
Katherine and Sylvia strolled among the families before the game started, leaves crunching nicely underfoot. They knew almost everybody and stopped to chat while the players got organized.
Her O'Dade cousins—Jed, David, and Brendan—lifted Sylvia off her feet in exuberant hugs. She fondly hugged back, her arms reaching around their big, bulky shoulders. Without siblings of her own, she'd been raised among these three bruisers. She attributed much of her own toughness to their rough and tumble play as children. They'd agreeably included her, and she'd worked hard to keep up with her slightly older cousins.
The guys were very excited about the game. Traditionally the teams were pretty evenly matched. Neither team had ever dominated, though the police had won the last three games.
It was payback time, now, Jed explained. The quarterback for the police team had been injured, sidelined for the last few weeks. The cousins loudly expressed their feigned sympathy for the unfortunate (and highly skilled) quarterback.

A certain amount of cash exchanged hands at the end of every game. This year, with the opponents' star quarterback on the injured list, the firefighters bet heavily. Sylvia's cousins expected to have their pockets well lined by the end of the game.

Katherine and Sylvia settled into their folding chairs alongside Russ and Marge O'Dade. Russ was Katherine's older brother, comfortable in his role of patriarch of the O'Dade clan. He'd been a steady presence for both Katherine and Sylvia in the years after Guy Huston's death and still was. Now, he sank back in his chair, happy with his cigar and a longneck bottle, while the women chatted.

Aunt Marge gave Sylvia a close inspection. She, too, was a nurse, as well as the provider of the chicken soup and brownies that had contributed to Sylvia's recuperation. She and Katherine had become friends many years ago, each fresh from nursing school in their first jobs at Memorial. One night they'd double-dated, Katherine with a cousin of Marge's, a young cop new on the beat, and Marge with Katherine's brother. Within months they were family.

She reached across Katherine to take Sylvia's hand, looking into her eyes. "How have you been doing?"

Sylvia smiled, knowing this no-nonsense woman wouldn't accept false reassurance. "My energy is nearly back—I've been working out a little, very gently. My crit is nearly normal again. Dr. Peterson sent me off with a clean bill of health when I saw him this week."

"Hmm. Your mother said you were back at work—up all night this week."

"Just the one night. I've had a lot of relief this week, and still have help scheduled next week, too."

"I'm sure your midwife friends are happy to help. You let them help you with call a little longer. I expect Marisel is taking care of you, too. I must say, I'm a little surprised to see her over there on the other side of the field."

Sylvia had been listening to Aunt Marge's instructions only marginally. She wasn't a huge football fan, but she enjoyed the sight of well-muscled men in snug jeans bent over the ball as much as any red-blooded woman. Play was underway now, and she was slightly distracted.

"Hmm? Marisel is here?" She looked across the field, spotted her there. "Oh. She's here with Emilio. I didn't know they were coming."

"Well, he's partners with your young man, isn't he?"

Sylvia bit back a groan. It was a surprisingly small family, surprisingly small town. "I don't have a young man, Aunt Marge."

Uncle Russ let out a bark. "Hah. That's his third sack. Maybe the boys should let up a little so we could see what he's got."

Sylvia turned her attention back to the game, where the RPD replacement quarterback was picking himself up, slowly. If she had it right, it was Jed who rolled off the QB so he could rise.

She looked over to Russ. "What who's got?"

Russ kept his eyes on the field. "Your young man."

"I don't have—I'm sorry?"

Cooper rolled his shoulder and tried not to limp as he walked off the field. Fourth down and they were kicking, with lost yardage on each play. He'd begun to think he was seeing double—or triple, more like it. Three blond heads sitting on top of steamrollers for bodies dominated the RFD's front line.

He was convinced the three took personal pleasure in bouncing him off the ground. Politely, they'd taken turns sacking him. None of them had given him a hand up, and each had snuck in an extra jab while they were down. Blond head on top, Cooper on the bottom, eating dirt.

The third time, he took a good look as the man rolled off him. Blue eyes met his, not friendly. Cooper became a little uneasy. He'd seen that face before.

Jackson had pulled him to his feet, kept his arm around him on the way to the sideline.

"Who are those guys?"

Jackson kept his eyes on the bench ahead. "What guys?"

"The three blond tanks."

"Uh, you must mean the O'Dades."

"They have something against me?"

Jackson hesitated. "Uh, you mean other than the fact that you're boinking their cousin? The one they treat like a little sister?"

Cooper stopped where he was, just off the field. He bent over, rested his hands on his thighs, hung his head, and took some breaths. That explained where he'd seen the last tank before—in a photo in Sylvie's office, with his arm wrapped around her shoulders. The photo that had sent a green streak of jealousy down Cooper's spine.

He straightened and turned slowly. He looked across the field and found them there—Sylvia sitting next to Katherine, and another couple, no doubt the two who'd spawned the three behemoths.

Her face was turned toward his, but she was too far away for him to be certain her eyes were on him. He thought they were, and was sure when he saw her hand reach out to clasp her mother's.

The kick was a good one, making up some of the yardage he'd lost. Jackson stood next to him, supportive hand still on his shoulder.

"Who was the last one, the biggest one?"

"Jed?"

"Tell the guys next time, let Jed through."

"*Let* him through?"

"Have they stopped any of them yet?"

"Well, they might have slowed them down a little."

Cooper watched the firefighters gain ground with steady short passes and runs. "Let him through."

✦ ✹ ✷

"Cooper's the new quarterback." Sylvia clung to her mother's hand, though her eyes were glued to the man across the field. She'd recognized the moment when he turned and sought her out in the crowd. She knew then that he'd learned it was her cousins who were making mincemeat of him.

"Uncle Russ, tell them to stop."

Russ took another pull on his bottle. "They're just playing ball, honey."

"No, they're not. They're defending my honor—at least, that's what they think they're doing, the big lugs. Make them stop. They're going to hurt him."

"He's a big boy, Syl. He wouldn't thank you for interfering."

"Mom—"

Katherine squeezed Sylvia's hand. "I'm afraid Russ is right, honey. It's a guy thing. We're not supposed to understand."

"Well, they're going to answer to me. I delivered every one of their babies."

"And a fine job you did with my grandchildren, too," Marge put in. "But what's your point? You just got done saying he's not your man. Though what you're thinking, I don't know. He looks mighty fine to me."

Russ took his eyes from the game to slant her a look until she continued.

"Not as fine as some, of course. Lacking a certain mature attractiveness."

Russ grunted and turned his attention back to the game while the women all exchanged smiles. Katherine offered Marge a quiet high five.

They all stood and cheered when the firemen scored on a long pass.

✦ ✹ ✶

At the hike from the center, Cooper dropped back fast. He handed the ball off to his running back, then lowered his shoulders and heaved forward. He met Jed just a little closer to the ground than the other man, pushed off, and found himself on top for a change, though the collision was just as painful.

He caught his breath for a minute then pushed up. Jed was still flat on his back, blood at his nose and surprise on his face. Still propping himself against one thigh, Cooper reached a hand down.

Jed wiped the blood from his nose, a little respect seeping into his face, before he met Cooper's hand. When Cooper pulled him up, their hands stayed clasped for a minute as they eyed each other.

"I'm going to see that she marries me. One day you and your brothers are going to have to explain to her children how you beat up on their old man."

Jed pulled at the waist of his tee shirt to swipe it over his face, leaving the grin in place. "I got no problem with that."

"You'll also have to tell them how I dumped you on your ass."

Jed had no more than a grunt for that.

Cooper nodded toward the sideline. "I got witnesses."

"Yeah? Well, it ain't gonna happen again." He turned and went back to the scrimmage line, his slowed movements giving Cooper significant satisfaction.

Cooper spent the next two downs making little gain but one by one putting the other O'Dades in the dirt. When he walked to the sidelines for the kick, Jackson and one of the running backs held him on his feet.

They held the firefighters to just a few forward yards on their possession.

When the RPD got the ball back, the offensive line held against the O'Dades. Cooper got his first pass off, a long one that got them to the firemen's twenty-yard line. On the next play, a hand off to Jackson, they scored.

Revenge was sweet, enough so that Cooper barely felt the pain of the celebratory hugs, slaps, and chest-bangs.

The score was still tied at the half. Though his teammates rowdily passed around the beer, Cooper spent the break on the bench, storing up energy. From that unsatisfying distance, he watched Sylvia. He was a little uneasy when she approached her cousins, to all appearances giving them hell. He shrugged it off, too beat to object to having a girl stand up for him.

The second half was a defensive battle. Passes were shut down with excellent coverage from both sides, and runs were held to short gains. Cooper wasn't sure if the O'Dades were taking it easier on him, or if he was just getting numb. He still spent a lot of time in the dirt and had trouble moving the ball downfield.

The RPD got the ball in the last two minutes on a quick-handed interception. Cooper limped onto the field with his teammates. Two successful runs brought them to mid-field. Then, on a spectacular Hail Mary pass to Jackson, they scored as the buzzer sounded.

Jubilant, the team carried Cooper and Jackson off the field. Laughing, celebrating, Cooper ducked his head as the traditional ice bucket was emptied over him. Sluicing it off, he straightened to shake hands as the firefighters filed past.

The two teams and their families combined forces for the

serious picnic that followed. Ribs slathered in Dinosaur Bar-
becue sauce sent out a spicy aroma from the grills, along
with sausages and hots. Women opened up baskets of
homemade fried chicken. There were large bowls of potato
salad, coleslaw and pasta. Cornbread and Italian rolls were
piled high on platters.

Cooper took a long pull from his first beer, enjoying the
cool slide of it down his throat. Emilio had a hand on his
shoulder, beaming like a proud father. He gloated about the
winnings he was about to collect.

Cooper searched the picnic area. The O'Dade family had
pulled a couple of picnic tables together and was clustered
there. He left Emilio's side and wandered in that direction.

Though the cops and firefighters mixed readily now, he
was surprised to find Lieutenant Sullivan standing with Sylvia, her mother, and another couple.

He was more surprised, in fact a bit apprehensive, when
Travis put his arm around Sylvia as Cooper approached.

He wanted to look at Sylvia, to fill his eyes with her, but
prudence had him nodding to Travis first.

"Nice game, Billings. You handled yourself well."

Cooper acknowledged that with another nod, sneaking a
look at Sylvia, who seemed entirely comfortable leaning into
the Lieutenant with her arm about his waist.

"I guess you know my goddaughter and her mother,
Katherine."

That had his eyes back on Sullivan, and his heart sinking.
"Goddaughter?"

"Yep. Her father Guy and I were partners many years
ago."

Cooper just kept himself from rolling his eyes, wondering
if he'd be looking for a new job soon. He girded himself,
keeping his eyes squarely on the sharp glare Sullivan was
sending him.

"I was there at the hospital, pacing with Guy the night
this little girl was born."

Cooper nodded some more, feeling neck deep in quick-
sand. He looked quickly to Sylvia and cursed her for the
amusement he saw on her face.

"Uncle T. claims he changed my diapers." She reached up
to kiss the man's cheek.

Katherine seemed to argue that with a huff. It appeared

to be an old, friendly controversy. Cooper noticed that the smile on Katherine's face seemed to be for Travis Sullivan alone.

Uncle T. Jesus. He cleared his throat, eyeing the Lieutenant. "I didn't know you were part of the family." Would not have anticipated it. Would have avoided it like the plague, if he could have. But he was in, and didn't want out.

The Lieutenant replied, with his eyes watching Katherine. "Well, not formally."

Cooper took a breath and gathered his courage. He leaned forward, put his lips on Sylvia's, lingered just a bit, just to make the point. He brushed his finger down her cheek, entirely too aware of how close that brought him to Lieutenant's hand at her shoulder. He wouldn't consider letting his mental shudder show. "How are you, sweetheart?"

She gave him a warm smile. "I'm fine." Her eyebrows raised a little as he took her arm and pulled. He kept his eyes locked with Sullivan's as he tugged her out of the older man's grip. Something passed between them when the Lieutenant let go, and Cooper acknowledged it. If he hurt Sylvia, he was a dead man.

He could accept that.

With Sylvia tucked into his side now, he turned to her mother. "Hello, Mrs. Huston."

He was very gratified when she went up on tiptoe to kiss his cheek. Bless the woman. "You didn't let those boys hurt you, did you?"

It was nice somebody cared. "No, ma'am, not so's you'd notice."

She stepped to his other side and took his arm. Maybe he was in love with the wrong woman. "This is my brother Russ O'Dade. He fathered those three giants you met today."

Katherine's hand still rested on his arm as he reached to shake hands. As expected, he fought a silent, manly duel against O'Dade's aggressive grip. The man was as big and tough as his sons, and prideful enough to subtly show it.

Cooper held back his grin of admiration. "Sir."

"You played a good game, son."

"I had help. Especially on the offensive front line."

"QB's gotta have protection."

Cooper nodded. "Particularly against the RFD."

Russ's pride was obvious now. "Yeah. My boys are tough.

Though I gotta say I've never seen anyone dump Jed that way."

This time Cooper let the grin show.

Russ put his arm around the woman at his side. "This is my wife, Marge."

Cooper nodded a greeting and was surprised when the attractive older woman reached up to pat his cheeks with both hands, then plant a kiss on his lips. He loved these women.

"So you're the one who's got Sylvia all hot and bothered."

He had to laugh out loud at that, and surreptitiously slid his hand down to give Sylvia a taunting pat on her bottom. "Yes, ma'am. I'm the one."

He laughed again when he took Sylvia's elbow in the rib—though it was an effort, as the rib was already no doubt bruised. He smiled down at her, extremely pleased.

Aunt Marge watched them, clearly enjoying the effects of her meddling. "Take him over to meet the boys and their families, honey. You don't want to hang around here with us old folks, I'm sure."

Sylvia acquiesced with a sharp look at Marge that made the older woman snicker. Cooper nodded to the group at they turned away and caught Marge's wink. He was still chuckling as Sylvia walked him toward a grill where her three O'Dade cousins appeared to be arguing over the ribs.

Before they got there, Cooper dug his heels in. "Wait a minute." He pulled Sylvia around until she faced him, question in her eyes, her back to her cousins. He waited until the three brothers paused in their discussion and looked over. Then he slid his arms around Sylvia and took her mouth.

She stiffened in surprise for a moment, but he coaxed with lips and tongue until she softened and leaned into him. He took the kiss deep as the wanting sneaked up on him. It was a long moment before he remembered his purpose.

He kept one hand on her back, bringing the pressure of her breasts against his chest. He took a minute to relish the pleasure of those firm mounds pressed against him.

Then he let his other hand slide down her back. It reached the end of her jacket then slipped over the tight jeans she wore. He opened his hand over her ass, massaging and squeezing, sliding just a little into her center.

He pulled her up against him but bit down on the urge to

grind against her. He didn't mind inflaming the cousins in front of him, in fact, he intended it, but he'd just as soon not give the older generation behind him cause to censure him. Or fire him.

Still, he took his pleasure, making it last. God, how he'd missed this woman in the last week.

He heard a feminine voice ahead of him murmur, "Oh, my." Slowly he loosened his grip and let Sylvia slide away. When his mouth let go of hers, she looked up at him, maybe a bit dazed but still sharp enough to give him a look. He was pretty sure she saw the humor.

"You're a devil, Cooper Billings."

"Maybe, but you're going to love me anyway."

"Maybe."

That response had him stopped dead again, reassessing her. Then he had his mouth on hers with no motive other than to celebrate that surge of hope she'd just given him.

When he pulled back, she spoke first. "Come on, let's go face your music. You've riled my cousins enough for one day."

He looked up, saw the three O'Dades champing for a piece of him. He noted that each one had an attractive blonde at his side, a hand on his arm, tethering. He was pretty sure that "Oh, my," had come from the blonde in the middle, and sent her a grin just in case.

He looked back at Sylvia one more time. "Okay. But we're going to talk about that 'maybe' later. Soon later."

He put his arm at her waist, and they walked toward the three couples.

Jed took an aggressive step forward, but the woman at his side, the one Cooper had shared the grin with, was quicker. She put out a hand and Cooper took it automatically. "I'm Theresa O'Dade."

Cooper nodded and spoke his name.

"I think you've kind of met my husband, Jed."

"Billings." It was said grudgingly, through clenched teeth. "O'Dade."

Sylvia and Theresa exchanged quick, worried looks before Theresa hurried on. "That's David and his wife, Madalyn. And Brendan and Marilyn." The women gave him warm smiles, a sharp contrast to their husbands' brusque nods.

Theresa continued. "If you think that Madalyn and Marilyn must be twins, you're entirely correct. So are David and

Brendan, for that matter."

Cooper nodded, relieved that it wasn't a head injury that had him seeing double.

"If you're done provoking them, we'd be happy for you to join us at our table. We have quite a few young ones around—feel free to just shove them out of your way."

It was true, Cooper saw. There must have been a dozen young blond heads, ranging from infants to a couple boys—also presumably twins, though maybe just cousins—of about ten years. Though he couldn't be sure about the one asleep in a stroller, bundled in Pooh blankets, it looked like they were all boys.

Some were paying serious attention to plates of hotdogs and hamburgers; others were wrestling with a couple golden labs, or generally doing light-hearted kid stuff that intrigued Cooper.

He thought about his own lonely and formal upbringing and was touched to his heart by this large, boisterous, and obviously happy family.

"You have beautiful families." He spoke to Theresa, but then looked at each of the men. They softened a bit, and Cooper knew then what their families meant to them. He saw Theresa nudge Jed.

Jed looked Cooper in the eye, acknowledging with a little attitude what Cooper had observed. His family was his weakness, and his wife could boss him around. With a mild show of reluctance, for form only, Cooper thought, Jed stepped forward and offered his hand. This grip was firm, but there was no challenge in it.

"You might wonder what you're getting into. No one would think you're a coward if you turned and ran just now. Or not much, anyway."

Cooper looked back steadily. "I'm staying."

Jed nodded. "Well, you're welcome, then."

That seemed to be that. David and Brendan also shook hands with Cooper, Brendan seeming especially friendly. "We enjoyed watching you knock Jed on his ass. We never could do it."

Jed cuffed his younger brother in mostly playful payback, though the kid made a show of pain. Chuckling, Cooper put his arm around Brendan and spoke seriously. "The big guys are slow. Like dinosaurs, you know, it takes a while for the signal to get to their brain. You just have to surprise them, do the unexpected. Then they're spitting grass out from between their teeth before they know what hit them."

They were all laughing even as Jed's shoulder knocked against Cooper and had him staggering into Brendan. He slanted Jed a look and said, "Ouch. I hurt."

Jed grinned happily and handed him a beer. "No doubt." But Cooper was pretty sure that under his breath, the man added, "pussy."

Sylvia apparently felt he was more or less safe. She gave his hand a squeeze before she left to join the women and do girl stuff with food and children.

Cooper followed the brothers in overloading their plates then pushing children aside to make room at the table. While they ate, they reviewed their favorite plays of the game, which, for most, involved putting Cooper on his ass. The three men patiently tolerated interruptions from their sons and mediated disputes as though routine.

Cooper enjoyed being a part of it, distracted only a bit by watching Sylvia interact with the women and kids. He knew he'd missed something when there was a pause in the conversation. He looked back to see three pairs of eyes on him.

David spoke. "He's got it bad, eh?"

Brendan nodded, clinked his bottle to Cooper's. "Yup. He's a goner."

Cooper eyed the three of them. "You all don't seem to be suffering too much for it."

Jed huffed. "Yeah, well, we got our women. Looks like you still have some work to do."

Cooper took a swig. "I'll get the job done." *And enjoy every minute of it,* but he was wise enough not to say that part out loud.

Jed might have read his mind, though. "That girl is like a sister to us."

Cooper nodded. "If I hurt her, I'm afraid you'll have to wait to kill me second. I'm pretty sure my boss will do the job first."

"True. Travis definitely has a thing for our Sylvie."

"And her mother?"

Jed paused, then nodded. "I think Katherine and Travis always had feelings, at least since Uncle Guy died. Travis was always there for Katherine and Sylvie. But nothing could come of it while Jill Sullivan lived."

Cooper knew Travis's wife had spent five years dying from breast cancer. The department had quietly sighed in relief when she'd finally been buried last spring. Word was she'd never made him happy.

Cooper followed Jed's gaze over to the grill, where the elder O'Dades and Katherine and Travis stood in line for ribs. Travis's hand gently touched Katherine's back.

Jed continued after he drained the last of his beer. "Maybe now that she's been gone for a while..." His eyes glimmered as he looked back to Cooper. "We think he's okay—for a cop."

"I think he's okay, too—for an Irishman."

That set up three loud objections, and next to him David shook up his beer to spray it over Cooper's head. Laughing, he knocked it away, then looked up to see Sylvia watching. Keeping his eyes on her, he spoke again. "You're right, though. I'm a goner."

That seemed to satisfy the brothers.

It was dusk when all the coolers had been packed back into truck beds and car trunks, the debris collected, and the little ones belted into car seats. Bets had been settled, the firefighters grumbling and the cops strutting.

A lot of people watched as Travis Sullivan escorted Katherine Huston to his car. Sylvia was one of them, though she looked up with a little smile when Cooper approached. He put his hand at her back, fingers fiddling with the tips of her hair, soft and rich.

"I think they love each other," she said quietly.

"You okay with that?"

"Oh, yes. My mother's been alone for so many years. And he's a good man."

Cooper just looked at her. "He's a cop."

"I know. I'm sorry. But it's different. He's at a desk."

He sighed, tried hard to let go of the bitterness. "Did you and your mother bring a car?"

"No, we rode with Russ and Marge."

He pulled her a little closer. "Let me give you a ride

home, then."

She looked up at him, searching his mood. He wondered what she saw. Inside him, frustration battled with desire. His urge to claim her, to make her his, warred with his own doubts. He hadn't forgotten he'd been the one to leave her waiting this week.

He dug for a smile. "We still have that 'maybe' to talk about."

She hesitated for just another moment. "Okay, I'll tell Uncle Russ to go on without me."

When she returned, they walked side by side to his car, arms encircling. He helped her in, then settled beside her. Neither spoke as he drove. He took her hand and held it against his chest, rubbing her palm.

At her house, he walked her to her door but stopped there and put his arms around her, drawing her close. "Tell me what it meant."

"When I said maybe?"

He nodded, his cheek resting against her hair.

She took a moment to answer. "That maybe you were right. Even if I didn't want it, or wasn't ready, I..." She took a breath, let it out on a sigh. "I have feelings for you, Cooper, deep ones."

He rocked her, grateful to his bones.

She lifted her head from his shoulder to look up at him. "How about you, though? You weren't very happy with me when you left on Monday."

"You mean that thing where you wouldn't give me your word about staying away from the gangs? That problem I have about being a cop, being a man, and wanting to keep my woman safe? That?"

She leaned back a bit further from him and lowered her gaze. He'd kept his voice quiet, but apparently his anger and frustration were less under control than he might wish.

"Yes, that."

He sighed, regretting the distance between them. "It's still a problem, Syl."

"I'm sorry, Coop." He knew she meant it. There was real regret in her voice.

"It's okay, baby." He pulled her back against him, despite her resistance. "We have time. We'll figure this out." They would, he swore. Or he'd die trying.

He held her until she slid her fingers along his neck, into his hair. He started kissing her. It was a long time before he stopped.

When he did, he tucked her into the house and waited for her to lock up. Then he walked to the car. Now, with no witnesses, he didn't bother to mask the limp.

Thorny relationship, gang problems, they'd have to wait. Tonight it was a hot tub and ibuprofen.

CHAPTER TEN

Wednesday afternoon, as the sun set, Marisel opened the door of Tynie's Place, stepped outside, then plopped down on one of the stairs, chin resting on her knees.

Sylvia put down her brush and wiped paint thinner off her hands. She'd been working to remove the graffiti that had appeared overnight—for the third time in a week. She went and sat next to her partner. They sat for a while, enjoying the quiet end of the day.

Then Sylvia spoke. "I thought I'd stop by Terry and Kiesha's place on my way in tomorrow, do the postpartum visit." She could feel Marisel's eyebrows raise without looking. Generally Marisel did the home visits, a check a few days after a birth to see how mom and baby were doing, to assess healing and make sure feeding was going okay.

Interest was in her voice. "I can do that."

Sylvia didn't meet her eyes. "I'd like to."

Marisel was quiet for a minute and Sylvia felt her scrutiny. "You want to talk to Terry. You're making a plan to deal with the gangs, aren't you?"

Sylvie had never been a good liar. "I am not. I just wanted to see Kiesha and him. I like them."

"You know if you try talking to the gangs, it's going to send Cooper. Emilio, too."

"I'm not living my life to please them."

Marisel turned to her, forced Sylvia to face her with her hands on her cheeks. "They want you to be safe. I do, too. Let them handle the gangs. Please, honey."

Sylvia pulled away. "I just want to see Kiesha and Terry." Marisel's silence—she was never silent—told Sylvia her friend was not convinced—and not happy. "How did your group go? Did anyone come?"

Marisel shrugged. "Two showed up. They didn't want to stay."

They watched down the street as the sun sank below the low cloud cover, visible for the first time since it rose that morning. Now it lit the street with a golden glow, the light nearly horizontal, casting long shadows. Its gleam made the crude slashes of paint almost pretty.

But nothing could pretty up the sentiment. The words were nasty, hurtful. They were about her. *Cop whore* was the least offensive. Mostly, she'd been reduced to crude designations of female body parts. Drawings were included, graphic depictions of male-dominated sexual acts.

The two boys who'd begun to add to the display last night were in the city jail now. Emilio and another cop had been waiting for them. It didn't make Sylvia feel any better.

The neighborhood had spent the last few days under siege. The gang response to the police arrests the prior week had been furious. Fast-paced violence surrounded the birth center.

One night the local grocer was robbed. The thieves, in black ski masks, brutally pistol-whipped old Mr. Wu. Sylvia went with teary, tottering Mrs. Wu to collect him from the ED, head stitched and bandaged. Later that night a brick was thrown through the front window of Tynie's Place.

The next night the neighborhood youth center was trashed, windows broken and equipment destroyed. Efforts to clean it up were slow—the building was abandoned as mothers kept their children home.

After dark, cars circled the block, windows open, vibrating with the beat of rap, spilling into the night words of violence against women and cops.

Young men loitered at the corners, smoking and listening to music. Each day, Sylvia and Marisel watched as girls on their way to the birth center were harassed, accosted. Mostly, they turned away. Boys coming onto the block were likely to lose their jackets, headphones, or other gear.

Sylvia sighed. Marisel's arm slipped around her, and she leaned into her friend. "What are we going to do?"

Marisel squeezed her tighter. "We're strong. We can survive this."

"I think maybe you and Lili and Antony should move out for a while."

"This is our home. I won't let them make us leave."

"I'm not sure it's safe here." The last rays of the sun

were gone now, and Sylvia shuddered against the cold.

Marisel stood. "We'll be okay. Cooper has someone here every night, remember? We have our own personal police protection."

Sylvia didn't know whether their protection was more help or harm. She was grateful for it, but she suspected it contributed to the missed appointments and lapse in attendance at groups.

She approached Cooper about it Thursday morning after a birth. He'd come in the early morning hours, relieving the officer who'd spent the earlier part of the night there, and dozed for a few hours on Sylvia's office couch.

When she heard him moving about in the bathroom, she took him a cup of coffee. He smiled his thanks as he accepted the coffee, gave her a soft kiss before he drank. "I used your toothbrush. At least, I hope it was yours."

"I think Curly keeps one in there." Curly was a very round, prematurely bald young man who helped with cleaning and heavy chores around Tynie's Place. While he worked, he practiced songs from his gospel choir in a lovely baritone voice. He hadn't shown up for his normal hours this week.

Sylvie grinned as Cooper swallowed his coffee with difficulty. "Ah. Thanks for that."

He kissed her again and pulled her to sit with him on the couch. He laid his head back and closed his eyes, his free hand clasping hers.

She meant to speak sternly with him, intending to negotiate an end to the police at her birth center every night. But she bit her tongue. He was drawn and tired. He was working extra hours in addition to sacrificing comfortable sleep to be at Tynie's Place. She knew he did it out of concern for her.

She stroked his rough beard, then leaned towards him, resting her head on his shoulder. She was quiet for a moment as he sipped his coffee.

"My patients aren't coming, Coop. They're missing appointments, missing groups."

He rubbed his thumb over the back of her hand. He was silent for a long moment. "You want me to stop coming here, to stop having a man here."

"Yes."

"No."

She bit back a frustrated moan. "The neighborhood feels like a war zone."

He opened his eyes, tipped his head to look at her. "It *is* a war zone. Are you blaming the police? Blaming me?"

"You know I'm not." She started to stand, but he held her arm. She searched his eyes, grief for this breach between them tearing at her heart. She tried to touch him, tried to soften what she had to say. His hard gaze stopped her.

"But many people here *are* blaming the police. When you arrested all those young men, many families were affected. Nearly everyone in the neighborhood had some connection— those boys are sons, grandsons, brothers, and cousins. And now the gang response has made things worse. That touches everyone. No one feels safe."

"No one was safe before. It was bad and getting worse. If people didn't realize that, they were living in a dream."

"It was *their* dream, Coop. Maybe it wasn't real, but it was theirs and they've lost it."

Cooper stood and paced in agitation. "Do you remember I told you that heroin is coming in now? There's a pattern to every city where the heroin market has opened up. Local gangs lose control to the heroin organization. Someone with a port connection takes over. He passes smack around like candy. He gets the locals hooked and then he has them.

"These small-time bullies we see on the street now, they're nothing compared to what we could see soon. They'll have military-like discipline and ruthless devotion to the organization. Mothers, sisters, girlfriends—they'll cease to matter. And the whole purpose will be profit. They'll be doing it all just to make the guy at the top filthy rich."

He came and sat next to her again, taking her hand. "Our goal is to break into it before the gangs are taken in. It's worked in a couple cities, where the cops broke up the gangs before a new organization could take hold. It's what we're trying to do. It's the only thing we know to do."

"And the neighborhood just has to suffer through it?"

He wanted to growl. "Yes."

"And Tynie's Place."

He paused. "Yes."

His voice raised in frustration as she turned away. He gestured to her desk. "You read. You must have seen reports of heroin-addicted babies born in cities like L.A., even Seattle."

It was true, she had. Heroin use was on the rise. People smoked it now instead of using needles, but it was still highly addictive. In major cities, neonatal intensive care units were developing protocols for infant withdrawal. Memorial was working on theirs.

"We'd like it if the neighborhood would trust us. We'll do everything we can to protect the people here. It would help if it looked like Tynie's Place trusted us."

She stood and walked to the window. He followed and put his hands on her shoulders. After a while she leaned back against him. "I trust you."

He kissed her temple. "Thank you, baby." He turned her and put his arms around her, took the kiss to her mouth. "I've gotta go. You going to go home and hit the sack?"

She nodded.

"I'm sorry I can't go with you. I'd like to help put you to sleep." He pulled her tightly to him, rubbed against her a little.

"Me, too. Guess I'll have to count sheep."

"How about tomorrow night? Will you be home?"

She was glad she had her head tucked into his shoulder as she thought about her arrangement with Terry. She remembered Cooper's words: *it's the only thing we know to do.* "I don't think so, not until late, anyway. I've got a meeting."

She tried to read what was in his pause and failed.

"Okay," he said, then, neutrally. "I'll give you a call on Saturday."

Friday afternoon Sylvia puttered in her office, waiting for Marisel to finish putting the place to rights after the day's activities. They'd had a fair showing for the prenatal group and several women kept their gyn appointments with Sylvia.

She'd encouraged Marisel to take the rest of the afternoon off, but the effort had been futile. Now she paced.

She was waiting for Terry to call, to tell her when she could meet with the Rocks. She needed the call to come when Marisel was away from the phone, and before Cooper or someone else showed up to spend the night. She needed the call to come before she lost her nerve.

She'd been shaking when she'd left the meeting with the Latin Kings. The protection she'd counted on—her relationship with the girls and women she took care of, the vigilant

concern she took to be sure women and babies made it safely through birth, the efforts to make family members and
babies' fathers feel welcome and included—all that had not
been enough to assure her safety. Or maybe only just.

But despite the shakes, she would meet with the Plymouth Rocks. She would fight for what was hers. A cushy birth
center in the suburbs was not what she wanted.

She snatched the telephone when the call came.

They would meet with her that night at ten.

The call woke Cooper just before ten. He was asleep on
the couch, the television still quietly playing a crime show.
He'd meant to stay awake to try again to reach Sylvia—she
hadn't been home when he called at eight, or at nine. But
days with so little sleep had taken their toll and he drifted off.

He fumbled the phone. "Billings."

"She's meeting with the Rocks."

It was Sunday. And even though it was pointless, even
though he knew, he had to ask. "She?"

"Your woman. The midwife."

"Now?"

"Yeah."

"Where?"

In the basement of a run-down apartment building. He
pulled his jacket on and slipped his cell into his pocket so he
could make calls on the way.

This time the leader was a man named C.J. Lawton. Sylvia knew of him—one of his children had been born at Tynie's
Place. He hadn't been there for the birth, however. He was
with another girlfriend, also pregnant.

He treated her much the same as Rosario had. He looked
her over with an assessing eye, blatantly communicating that
he had only one use for women. He waved a dismissive hand
when she made her appeal.

"Why you think I'd care about your place?"

"Claudia might care. She gave birth to your son there."

"Claudia know how to mind her own business. She know the way for a bitch to act."

And she, Sylvia, did not, was the clear implication.

C.J. moved to her, put his hand on her throat and lifted so she went up on her toes. His eyes leering, he put his other hand on her breast and squeezed roughly.

Biting back a moan of pain and fear, she tried to pull away. His hand tightened on her throat. Nearing panic, she prayed that some of the young men present who knew her would stand for her. But everyone was quiet around them, watching. Sylvia felt an obscene interest rise. Then there was a distraction of footsteps at the stairs.

C.J. turned his head. "Shit," he said. "Search him."

There was movement to her side, out of her line of vision. Then she heard Cooper's voice.

"Take your hands off her, C.J."

C.J.'s eyes went back to her for a moment, and she saw the malicious gleam. He kept his hand at her throat but loosened it enough so she could turn her head.

She saw Cooper glance around the room, his eyes barely touching on Sylvia, but she knew he'd just taken in every detail—the number and position of the gang members, the presence of weapons, the fact that she was as yet unharmed.

"Pig. Your bitch came to see me."

Cooper's voice was hard. "Take your hands off her, now."

C.J. met his glare with apparent indifference. He tightened the hand at her throat. Then he leaned over her and ran his tongue across her mouth.

Cooper pushed forward. Several handguns came out. He stopped, hands up.

C.J. smiled in evil pleasure. "She taste good."

"C.J., if you touch her again, I will kill you." It was a certain statement of fact, and Sylvia was sure everyone who heard it had no trouble believing it. The excess of guns pointed at him seemed to matter not at all.

C.J. kept his hand at her throat, but pushed her back half a step. "Your bitch don't know her place."

Now Cooper's gaze did rest on Sylvia for a long few seconds. "It's a problem."

"She make it my problem."

"No. It's not your problem."

C.J. shrugged. "She here to negotiate with me. In front of my men."

"You and I will negotiate later. She leaves with me now."

"The Rochester Police will bargain with me?"

"This is personal, C.J., not business."

"It business to me."

"We'll have this disagreement later. I'm taking her now."

Hands still lifted at his side, Cooper walked to them and stood behind Sylvia. He kept his eyes on C.J. while he put his arm between them, his forearm spanning her shoulders just below C.J.'s hand. He stepped back, keeping her held against him.

C.J. reddened slightly, his eyes hard, but he let her go. "This ain't done."

Cooper answered softly. "No, it's not." Then he had a hand on her arm and one at her back, and he pushed her to the stairs.

✦ ✹ ✧

Outside icy snow fell. Cooper took her through the door and down the side steps. Emilio was there, pressed beside the door. Sylvia saw Cooper give him a signal. He fell in behind them as they strode to the parking lot.

Sylvia knew she was in trouble, and matters got worse when she saw her three cousins leaning against Jed's car, parked haphazardly at the curb, engine running. She spoke when Cooper pushed her closer. "Jed, what are you guys doing here?"

"Wrong question, Sylvie. What the hell are *you* doing here?"

Sylvia gulped. She'd heard that question in her mind a million times. Generally it was Cooper speaking, but it had that same outraged tone.

She looked up at Cooper. He glared at her, clearly leashing his temper. "I thought I might need help. I called them and they came." He pounded fists with Jed.

He started to speak again, then interrupted himself as Emilio let out a curse. "What is it?"

Emilio watched the corner of the building, where a couple of the young men from the basement were just disappearing. Emilio started to move, even as he answered. "That was Terry."

He took off on a run. Cooper pushed her one step further, into Jed's hands.

She reached back. "Cooper."

He gave her a short, hard look. "Later. Take her home, Jed." Then he, too, disappeared around the corner of the apartment complex.

The boys realized they were being followed and broke into a run. When they split up, Cooper and Emilio followed the gray polar jacket that Terry had been wearing. They ran for several blocks but lost him in an alley when the kid went up a fire escape and took the ladder with him.

Emilio cursed roundly as they walked back to their cars. "This will kill my sister. Already her son is dead from gangs. I think I'll kill Terry myself."

Cooper walked with a hand on his partner's shoulder, aware of the responsibility he felt for the boy. Emilio's sister, Hildie, had taken him into her heart, her home. Emilio spent time with him, too, made sure he went to school and had a life outside of the streets.

"He's got his own child now. What the hell is he thinking?"

When they reached their cars, Cooper offered to go with him to Hildie's house. Emilio nodded his appreciation, but sent him off to deal with his own large problem—that being one Sylvia Huston.

Cooper silently wished him luck and started slowly driving to Sylvia's. He reviewed the confrontation with the Rocks, feeling endless gratitude toward Sunday for that phone call.

Then he pulled over and sat flicking a fingernail against his teeth. He took out his cell phone and dialed the number that had popped on his caller ID when Sunday had called. It rang twice.

"Yeah."

"Terry?"

There was a pause. "Yeah. Who is this?"

Cooper closed the phone and turned his car around.

He pulled up in front of Hildie's duplex. Emilio's car was in the drive and the lower level of the house, where Hildie and Terry lived, was lit. Upstairs a baby cried.

He heard the sounds of distress as he stepped onto the porch—Hildie wailing, Emilio yelling angrily. He didn't bother to knock—it wouldn't be heard anyway.

He pushed through the door and saw that Emilio had Terry by the jacket, slammed up against the wall. He went up behind his partner, grabbed his shoulder and started to pull him back.

Emilio tried to shrug him off. "Get the hell out of here, Coop."

"You're about to beat the crap out of our best source, partner."

Terry met his eyes over Emilio's shoulder and lifted his head. Emilio stood down just a little. "What are you talking about?"

"He's Sunday, Emilio. He's on our side."

Emilio still held Terry's jacket, but not in anger now. "That true, Ter?"

Terry looked at Emilio and after a while he nodded once. Emilio let him go and turned away while Hildie went to Terry. She brushed at his cheek, ruffled her hand over his head. "Are you in the gang, Terry?"

Taller than Hildie, Terry put his arm around her and squeezed. "No. You know I wouldn't do that."

She turned in his arms to look at her brother. "What are you talking about, Emilio?"

He ran his hands over his face. "He's been calling Cooper and me, informing on the gang."

"What?"

"He's been—spying."

Hildie's face paled as she understood. She looked back to her adopted son. "No more. It's too dangerous."

Terry looked at Emilio. "C.J. Lawton killed Eric." He said it as though that explained everything, as though it was enough. And it was.

Emilio nodded. "All right. We'll find a way to bring him down for it. But Hildie's right. What you've been doing is too dangerous. It ends, here and now."

"No. Not until it's finished."

Cooper went to him, put his hand on his shoulder. "It *is*

finished, Terry. Lawton is going to fry."

Terry watched Cooper for a long minute, then nodded. "Okay."

Hildie's tears started again. She pulled Emilio into her arms as well.

Cooper left the three of them together, but not before he solemnly shook Terry's hand.

CHAPTER ELEVEN

Sylvia was in bed, but far from sleep, when the knock at her door came. She knew it was Cooper. She'd been expecting him, wondering what she faced now. It was the wondering that had kept her awake. The knock was not reassuring; he wasn't gentle about it.

She pulled a robe over her silk gown and went downstairs, turning on a couple of lights along the way. The front porch light was on, and she could see his shadow through the amber-colored panes of the door. She turned the single lock and began to open it.

Cooper slammed his hand against it, causing it to burst open. Sylvia jumped back in alarm.

He stepped through, shoving the door closed behind him, his eyes sharp on her as he locked it. "You didn't know who was there. Never open a door without knowing who's behind it."

She took a moment to gauge his mood. It wasn't exactly what she expected. He was angry and obviously determined to make it known. But there was something else, too. Satisfaction, maybe. Something that seemed to please him. "I knew it was you."

"You thought you knew. You didn't check it out. I'll say it again. Never open a door without knowing who's behind it." He lifted his hand, signaling her to stop as she began another objection. "There's only one thing for you to say. Say, 'Yes, Cooper.'"

She backed away a little, still trying to assess. Finally, she caved. He had the right to object to her behavior tonight. "Yes, Cooper."

He took a step toward her, looming. "Never walk to your car alone. Never drive without locking all the car doors." He paused, waiting.

Ah. Safety Lessons 101. After a moment she got what

the pause was about and took her cue. "Yes, Cooper." Still, she was uncertain about him and took another step back.

He followed her again. "Keep your cell phone with you all the time. Not just in your purse. In your hand or at your side."

"Yes, Cooper." She continued to back up, moving toward the living room.

This time when he stepped forward, he lifted a finger and pointed toward the stairs. He unzipped his jacket and dropped it on a chair.

That explained the glitter in his eyes. Her body quickened, knowing what was coming, anxious to feel his touch again. She trembled a little, but her next step back was in the direction of the stairs.

He stalked, matching her step for step until she backed into the stairs. She felt with her bare foot and went up two steps. For a moment, she topped him, and she felt a little safer. But he watched her with predatory eyes, then unbuttoned his shirt and followed her to the first step.

Her breath came quicker. She backed up another step, away from the heat of his body.

"Take off your robe."

With trembling fingers, she grasped the edges of her robe, but more in an instinctive effort to keep it closed than to open it.

His eyes gleamed as he advanced again. "Do it. And say, 'Yes, Coop.'"

She went up another couple steps as she gathered her courage. On a breath, she opened her robe and slipped out of it. She draped it over the banister and it slid down until he stopped it with his hand.

She stood, trying to keep her body still, while he studied her. She heard his breathing become strained. Fire blazed wherever his gaze touched. It fell to her breasts and held there until her nipples tightened. His eyes glinted in satisfaction and then went lower, where she knew he could see the dark shadow of her mound behind the sheer white silk. Wildly, she imagined he could almost see the dampening of her center there. Nostrils flaring, he drew a breath, scenting her.

Then his eyes came back to hers. "You forgot to say, 'Yes, Coop.'"

"Yes, Coop." It came out in a whisper.

Slowly, she backed up the stairs. He kept pace.

Then he began talking again, and she shook her head, trying to clear it in order to follow.

"If you're in a situation where there's gunfire, get down. Hit the ground, stay down, and cover your head. If you can get to cover, do that, but most important, stay down. And cover your head."

A moment of clarity pierced the sexual onslaught that had disrupted her ability to think. Suddenly, she understood. He accepted that he wouldn't be able to keep her safe by limiting her behavior. He chose another way to satisfy his need to protect her.

This time, she smiled as she waited for his prompt.

"Say, 'Yes...dear.'"

She'd reached the top of the stairs and began backing into her room. "Yes, dear."

That brought a feral smile from him. He tore off his shirt, tossing it carelessly over the rail, seeming unconcerned that it fell to the floor below. He followed her into the bedroom. His hand moved to the fastening of his jeans as she backed against the bed. Anticipation had her quivering. Her hands itched to reach out and stroke the hard surfaces of his chest.

"If we're in a situation together, I want you behind me. Touch me so I know where you are, but don't hold me in case I have to move."

"Yes..."

He hesitated at her pause, considering. "Darling."

"Darling."

He smiled again. "Lie back on the bed."

Silently, she complied.

"Pull up your gown. Open your legs."

Breath catching, she did as he instructed. A growl of satisfaction sounded deep in his throat as his eyes focused on her center, revealed by the spread of her thighs.

"More."

She opened herself wider. Gaze still on her core, he slid his jeans to the floor. When he straightened, she saw how hard he was, jutting out, pulsing.

He loomed over her, covering her without touching. He held himself with an elbow beside her head, and his knees between her legs, separating, bracing her open. Exposed, racked with sharp longing, she moaned.

He waited until her attention came back to his face. "Hostage situation. Remember, if he needs you as a hostage, he won't want to hurt you. At the least, he won't kill you. If he leaves with you, we lose control. Don't let it happen. If he tries to take you, sink to the floor as though you've fainted. He'll have trouble managing you and his weapon, too. That will give us a chance to take him."

He put his hand on her breast, lifting it toward his mouth. "Say, 'Yes, my love.'"

She closed her eyes, almost cried it out. "Yes, my love."

As the words were spoken, he took her nipple, still covered in silk, sucking it hard into his mouth. Just that one hard pull and then he let her go, not touching again, his eyes fixed on her nipple that she knew was visible now through wet silk.

With his free hand, he reached down and then he was prodding, pressing at her opening. He sank in just a little. She shuddered as he stretched her to accommodate his size. Slowly, he penetrated, a little further. She writhed beneath him, almost feeling pain, but wanting, needing more.

Yet he held back, watching her, knowing her need. "You love me, Sylvia. Say it."

"Yes."

He pushed a little further. "Say it."

"I love you, Cooper."

Slowly, he slid into her, all the way, until she was pinned between him and the bed, her legs wide, stayed there by his shaft deep inside her.

Still holding himself above her, he took her face in one hand, his thumb along her jaw, keeping their gazes locked. "You're mine, now."

He waited, and she nodded.

With exquisite intention, he slid out of her and then in again, all the way, and held. "You took a bigger chance tonight than I've ever taken as a cop. You wanted to protect something important and were willing risk your life. If I can live with that, so can you. I'll be careful on the job. I promise. I want to come home to you every night for the next fifty years. But neither of us can make the risk go away. We just have to accept it and love each other anyway."

He moved in her, ever so slowly, pulling out and then penetrating, still looking into her eyes, not otherwise touching.

She understood now the glimmer of satisfaction she'd seen when he barged his way into her house. Her actions had nullified her right to object to his work. With more hope than regret, she let go of the restraints she'd placed on her heart.

In moments, thought was gone. He began to move with force. Heat rose, burning. Her body arched of its own accord. Satisfaction would be hers, too. She raised a hand to his face, slid fingers into his hair, caressing, wanting. "Yes."

She brought his head down until their mouths touched. It was a touch that broke the storm he'd been holding back. His weight pressed against her as he used both hands to roam her body. His tongue sank into her mouth, seeking the taste of her, finding soft corners, plumbing her depths.

His hands urgently stroked the length of her, leaving marks with their strength, heating her with their friction. He ran them back up her sides to take her breasts. Encircling, he squeezed and molded. Then he took her peaks, tugging, pulling, rubbing them through the silk against the bristly hair of his chest. He tore at her gown to bare one mound and took it with his mouth.

His hips pistoned as he pounded into her. One hand left her breast to slip beneath her, gripping her ass, securing her for his thrusts. He tipped her toward him and grunted in gratification as he reached her core. He ground into her, guttural moans escaping his throat. "Baby."

He slid his middle finger down her center, circling where he'd never touched before.

"No," she said, "not—"

But he pressed in, a breach that was rough and primitive and taking. Wailing, Sylvia dug her heels into the bed and arched up against him, meeting and answering each plunge. Each movement increased the stimulation from that wicked finger. She cried out again, and ran her hands ran down his back, sliding over sweat-slicked muscle, digging for purchase with nails.

They strained against each other, breath coming in harsh gasps, muscles rigid, bodies heaving in the quest for fulfillment. They found it together, he filling her with hot spasms, she taking him, accepting him, in a throaty scream.

He continued to thrust as the orgasm stretched out, holding them both in long minutes of ecstasy. Even when it was over, when he collapsed finally on top of her, their hands continued to seek, their bodies still let out small shudders.

Finally, he withdrew. He rolled a little to her side, taking only enough of his weight away to let her breathe. He pulled blankets up over them and tucked pillows under their heads. Then he sank down, his arms around her, his thigh between hers, his lips touching her neck.

"Sylvia. Please. Don't ever put yourself in danger like that again."

"Please, Cooper, keep yourself safe."

"Okay."

"Okay."

It was still dark when his movement woke her. She was on her side with him curled behind her. Her upper thigh was lifted, opening her. She didn't know if she'd slept like that, or if he'd positioned her that way.

He rubbed himself between her legs, stroking against her. He slid along her cleft, picking up the moisture that was still there from their last coupling. Then he pressed further, generating a hot friction over the little nub that was the center of her pleasure.

The strokes continued, harder, more insistent. His breath came as a hot rasp against her shoulder.

She curled her fingers into the sheet beneath her hand and let out a moan.

Cooper slid his left arm under her, bringing his forearm across her chest, and covered her right breast with his hand. His other hand squeezed at her ass, opening her wider, making her more vulnerable to his strokes. Then he gripped her hip and rolled with her so she was flat on her belly.

He put his weight fully on her. Between her legs, he prodded, then found her opening and sank into her. With long thrusts he filled her. He slipped his right hand underneath her, caressing with his fingers at her center.

Grunting and moaning his pleasure, he moved with more power. Each time he came into her, the force of his thrust moved her against his hands. Her breasts rubbed against him, one pressed and chafed by his forearm, the other in his hand, pulling against the hold he had on her nipple. Between her legs, she was brought harder and harder against the pressure of his fingers.

She arched a little to meet his thrusts, then cried out as each time she was driven back into the possession of his fingers. She was taken by his hunger, lost in need. She was his, entirely.

She felt his teeth scrape at her shoulder. He pinched, tugging at her nipple, and lifted her hips a little off the bed as his fingers delved harder. She screamed as she came with the next thrust and he strained into her, rocking, extending her orgasm. Then he let out a rough cry as he pumped into her, emptying himself.

Their breath came in frantic gasps, almost fearful, as they gradually found themselves again. His hands moved to cover hers where they fisted on the bed. Their fingers entwined and clutched. Without otherwise moving, without speaking, they slept.

Early in the morning, she felt him leave her bed. He kept the lights out as he moved to the bathroom and started the shower. She rolled over, snuggling into the warmth still there from his presence. Her body gently thrummed, satisfied and mildly sore in the areas that had been the focal points of his attention.

He came out of the bathroom, leaving the door open a crack for light. He opened it more when he saw she was awake. He kept glancing toward her as he slipped into his boxers and jeans, then sat on the bed to pull on his socks and boots. That was the extent of his clothing that had made it as far as the bedroom.

When he was done, he leaned over, searching her eyes for a moment, then kissed her. "I've got to go to work."

He hadn't smiled, but she did as she put her hand on his cheek. "Me too, in a bit."

Still watching her, he gave her a small grin as he rubbed his cheek against her palm. "I used your razor. Your shaving cream is kind of girly."

"I'll get some more manly stuff if you want."

"I do want. I want to stay with you, or you with me."

"Is this about keeping safe, or about our relationship?"

"You don't think you're going to scare me off using that

word, do you?"

"Relationship?"

"Yeah. It won't work." He nuzzled into her a little. "Will you marry me, Sylvie?"

Her heart flipped, full of hope and longing and fear. "Cooper."

He lifted his head, smile gone now as he watched her, waiting. After a moment his brow rose, maybe a bit imperiously.

She bit back a laugh. She wanted to throw her arms around him in celebration, but she still struggled to let go of the fear that encased her heart. *Choose hope*, she told herself. In the end, it was simple. "Yes."

He held her face and watched her a bit longer, then kissed her gently. "Good. Thank you. I love you."

"I love you, too." Their kiss became more and they held each other, arms tight, hands grasping, soothing.

He pulled back after a minute. "However, about keeping you safe—"

She stifled a sigh. "Yes?"

"Were you planning to meet with the Latin Kings, too?"

"Uh—"

"Jesus, you already have, haven't you?"

She thought better of answering. He dropped against her, forehead to forehead, letting out a groan.

"Jorge Rosario?"

Reluctantly, she nodded.

"I'm trying hard not to think about where he put his hands on you."

She slipped her hand into his hair, stroking. "He didn't touch me."

"Can we agree that you won't do anything like this again, without telling me beforehand?"

He lifted his head to capture her gaze before she answered.

She answered without hesitation. "Yes."

He closed his eyes for a minute, then turned to sit beside her, securing her close with his arm. She tugged at the sheet to keep herself covered.

"What deal did you try to make?"

"A three-block radius around Tynie's Place as a safe zone. If anything happens in that area, I'll close for three days. If it keeps up, I'll close permanently and move to the suburbs."

"I could live with that, though I have to say it sounds like an empty threat."

"Maybe. They don't know that."

"Did Jorge give you an answer?"

"No. I didn't really expect one. He has no reason to care about Tynie's Place. I just hoped that once the girls heard about it, they'd put some pressure on the guys. I don't have any idea if it will be enough."

"Was there a plan for meeting again? How was he going to give you an answer?"

"No plan. I hoped he'd contact me."

Cooper ran his hand over his face. "Yeah, that's something to hope for, all right."

Sylvia elbowed him.

He took it with a minor grunt, indulging her. "Did you get any sense that he didn't have the power to make a deal with you?"

"You mean, that he'd have to run it past someone else?"

He nodded, still watching her.

She considered. "I don't think so. He sort of implied..."

He took a deep breath, his hand tightening where it stroked her arm. "That he'd be willing to carry on negotiations after a good f—"

She stopped him with her fingers to his mouth, but his eyes communicated both the end of the sentence and his anger. Their gazes battled until finally he relented with a long sigh.

"I think C.J.'s hands are tied. I think he's lost control."

"That there's a takeover, you mean."

"Yeah."

"How much evidence do you have?"

"Not evidence. Just a lot of indicators." He lifted his fingers to her chin. He held her gaze, considering. "We think it may be Parsons."

"Noah Parsons?"

"A lot of things fit. And remember, it got a lot worse for Tynie's Place after you turned him down."

It seemed impossible that a city councilman would make himself a gang lord. She replayed the events in her mind and recalled the touch of his hand on her throat. She shuddered as she realized it could be true. "It's about drugs, isn't it? The heroin."

"Baltimore is a major port. I think he had connections while he was there."

"You think he was the one you were after that night your partner was wounded, don't you?"

Cooper nodded and pulled her tighter into his arms. "And you, my love, have dissed him." His lips touched her temple. "It's business to him—organizing the Rocks, controlling the neighborhood, developing a marketing system for the drugs. But you made it personal."

She shivered again, cold even in his arms. His hand stroked her face before he gently kissed her. "Please be very careful. Don't be alone at the birth center, ever. Call me any-time. Use my cell, or my pager if I don't answer right away. Program my numbers into your phone."

She nodded, but he still wasn't satisfied. He held her face, gazes locked. "*Will* you be very careful? Can I trust you to not take any chances with your safety?"

She read the need in his eyes. She cupped his cheek, then touched her lips to his. "Yes."

CHAPTER TWELVE

Cooper sped on his way to the office, but Emilio was already at his desk. A raised eyebrow informed him that his partner noted his tardiness. Luckily, he'd had the foresight to bring doughnuts and real coffee.

By mid-morning, they turned in a written report to Sullivan. As was proper, they documented their interaction with the Plymouth Rocks and proposed a follow-up plan of action. The details they'd omitted, such as the identity of the civilians present, could be seen as reasonable editing. They hoped.

By afternoon, they'd spent two hours with Terry. Though they wouldn't put him on the streets again, they still could use his knowledge. They wanted two things: to close the case on C.J. Lawton for Eric's murder, and to establish Noah Parsons's role as ganglord/druglord. But Terry wasn't high enough up in the Rocks organization to have ever seen a council meeting, ever heard a murmur about Parsons. They needed another line, someone closer to the top.

They'd run out of ideas and were beginning to spin wheels. With a sudden thought, Cooper looked at Terry.

"Who killed Tomas Andujar?"

Terry raised his eyebrows. "You just want a name? You always say you want a name and a case."

"This time I just want a name."

"I heard it was Dwight Folsom. He was a friend of Antwan's."

Cooper gestured to Emilio. "Let's go pick up Dwight."

Emilio hesitated. "We don't have anything on him."

Cooper gave a small smile. "We're not going to arrest him. We're going to protect him."

His partner answered with a slow grin. "Okay."

A half-hour later, they had an apartment address and a favorite hangout for Dwight. They were heading out when they were waylaid by a call into Sullivan's office. He left them standing, scrutinizing them with obvious suspicion. Cooper forced himself to stand still, to show no fear as the lieutenant paged through their report.

"You were told of this gang meeting by an informant."

"Yes, sir." The words came out of Cooper and Emilio at the same moment, but not very strong for all that.

The lieutenant's sharp eyes focused on Cooper. "And the reason you felt compelled to enter the building alone was..."

Cooper caught himself shuffling and silently cursed. "We were warned of a potential threat to a civilian."

"And you removed said civilian to safety?"

"Yes, sir."

"You're currently working to obtain further intelligence from your informant?"

Emilio fielded that one. "We've done that already, sir. We're just short of bringing in C.J. Lawton for the murder of my nephew three years ago." He paused and shared a glance with Cooper.

Travis caught it. "And?"

Cooper nodded and Emilio continued. "We think we're going to find it's Councilman Parsons behind the Rocks reorganization. Coop's been in touch with his old Baltimore office. We're pretty sure Parsons is trying to run heroin."

Their boss sat back, scrubbed his hands over his face. "You can't know how much I didn't want to hear you say that." Nothing was messier for a police force than to go after a charismatic local politician. "You won't make any mistakes on this, right?"

The partners vowed quietly, "No, sir."

"Good. We owe a debt to your informant."

"Yes, sir."

"Dismissed."

Cooper and Emilio exchanged a quick glance of relief and turned to the door.

"Billings."

Cooper turned back. The sense of relief had been premature. He watched with regret as Emilio, smirk on his face, left him alone with Sullivan.

"The next time this civilian gets herself in trouble, I want to hear about it then, not the next day."

Cooper met the Lieutenant's blue eyes. "Yes, sir. I'm

planning that there won't be a next time."

Travis gave him a skeptical look. "Huh." He leaned back, motioned Cooper into one of the chairs that faced his desk. "Katherine Huston has agreed to marry me."

That sent a shiver down his spine, but he found, despite it, a genuine smile. "Congratulations, sir. She's a good woman."

Sullivan sat with his hands over a belly still hard with muscle, just a little extra fat. He was the epitome of watchful waiting.

Finally, Cooper broke. "Uh, her daughter has agreed to marry me."

Sullivan smiled, too, but it was a little scary. "Guess that will make me your father-in-law."

There went that shiver again. "Yes, sir."

The grimness with which he said that brought a deep laugh out of the lieutenant. He stood and came around the desk. Cooper stood, too, and found himself warmly embraced.

"She couldn't do better, son."

"Thank you, sir."

Sullivan patted his back one more time, then held a grip with just a little pressure on his shoulder. "But, still..."

"Yes, sir. If I hurt her, I'm dead."

"That's my boy."

Dwight Folsom's apartment was empty, so Cooper and Emilio headed to the dive where he was supposed to hang out. Emilio's eyes scanned the streets as he drove. "Sullivan is solid."

Cooper nodded. Not every lieutenant would back up his officers, without question, in the face of such politically volatile charges.

"Still, he'll have our butts if we screw up."

"Oh, yeah."

Emilio went in the front door of Sloe Ginny's and flushed out Dwight. The young man plowed into Cooper, who'd covered the back door. He took the kid by the collar and walked him back into the bar. The three took a table in a dark corner.

Dwight pulled his hood up over his head and scrunched low in his chair. While Ginny, ebony-skinned and sporting white support stockings, shuffled over with their beers,

Cooper pondered the vagaries of a life in which a scum like Folsom didn't want to be seen with *him*.

Emilio spoke. "We heard a rumor that you took out To-mas Andujar."

Folsom spoke to his beer. "Pigs make arrests 'cause of rumors, now?"

"Point is, if we heard the rumor, probably other people did, too."

Cooper picked up the story. "Yeah. Like the guy who did your buddy, Antwan."

"Kings did Antwan."

"You think? Antwan invited a couple of the Kings into his place, sat and watched videos, drank a couple of forty-ouncers with them, before they popped him?"

Emilio leaned forward. "Dwight, the Kings didn't do Ant-wan."

The punk lifted his head, searched Emilio's eyes. "Who, then?"

"Antwan took a shot at Alejandro Perez. It was unsanc-tioned. Who would want to make a point about that?"

Dwight shrugged. "Don't know what you mean."

Cooper thunked a finger against the boy's forehead. "You'd better think about what we mean, 'cause you just made an unsanctioned hit, too, didn't you?"

He spoke to Emilio. "The kid's in trouble, and he's too stupid to know it."

"Yeah. He's already dead." Emilio shrugged, then contin-ued. "Dwight, you didn't dump Tomas on the steps at Tynie's Place. Haven't you wondered how he got there?"

Cooper nudged his partner's arm. "I figure one of his pals saw the shooting. He played it smart, made a call. Probably C.J. C.J.'s pissed—the council is supposed to approve hits now."

Emilio nodded. "Yeah. C.J.'s pissed. He don't look so good, like he's not in control of his gang. He's lost face. So he takes advantage of the situation, tries to turn it his way. He has To-mas dumped at the birth center. Still, he can't be happy."

"C.J.'s kind of like a bee—you don't want to make him mad. Know what I mean?" Cooper turned back to Dwight. "We'll make sure they take real good care of you in the morgue, keep your shriveled little dick respectfully covered."

Emilio started to rise. "Good luck, son."

Dwight stopped him, fear in his eyes now. "Can you help me?"

Emilio shook his head. "Not much. I gave Mrs. Andujar my word I'd bring in her son's killer."

"What do you want?"

"C.J."

"It ain't just him, man."

"Someone's making a play for control of the Rocks?"

Under the hood, Dwight's head nodded.

"Councilman Parsons?"

Hesitation, then another nod.

Cooper and Emilio exchanged a look. Cooper spoke. "You get us him, you cop a plea for Tomas, we'll do what we can for short time."

"No time."

"Never happen."

"All right, then. Short time."

Cooper and Emilio ran late in a meeting with CID and representatives from the D.A.'s office. Sullivan had approved their plan for constructing a net around Parsons and had called in the captain. After a heated debate, they'd agreed to leave the chief out of it.

They put Dwight in a safe house. They would need him when the time came to bait the trap.

Emilio was happier than he'd been in three years. If C.J. Lawton got caught up in the same snare with Parsons, he would feel he'd done what he could for his sister. And Terry was doing okay. They'd talked about the possibility that Terry would pursue training as a medical examiner. Sullivan said there'd be a Police Fund scholarship for him if he wanted it.

He'd run into Sylvia as she was locking up the birth center. He walked her to her car, saw her locked safely inside. She was on her way to Cooper's place, on call but having a quiet night so far.

Now he stood outside Marisel's door. He heard activity inside and knew she wasn't alone. Well, it was past time he met her daughter.

He knocked and Lilibeth answered. She had a baby on her hip, a little boy with dark curls, deep brown eyes and thick lashes, just like his mother and grandmother. Lilibeth looked him up and down, then lifted her brow in question.

"I am Emilio Navarre. I'm here to see your mother."

The brow lifted a bit higher. "*Momentito*." She stood in front of him, hand still holding the door and turned her head. "*Mama! Para ti.*"

She shifted the baby on her hip and watched not Emilio, but the door to the kitchen. Marisel appeared there, face flush from working at the stove, by the smell of it. She wiped her hands on a towel.

"*Si*? Oh." She paled just a little, but he liked the way she brushed nervous fingers through her hair and tried to straighten her skirt under the apron she wore. "Emilio."

Lilibeth's surprised eyes were on his now, and he knew she could see heat there.

"Mari."

She stepped a little closer, but still was most of the way across the room. "Come in, please. This is my daughter, Lilibeth, and her Antony. Lili, this is *Detectivo* Navarre." She paused, fingers nervously bunching her apron. "He is Investigator Billings's partner."

He knew she could see the hurt that limited introduction caused him. She covered her mouth with her hand in a gesture of regret and uncertainty. He watched her another moment, then took matters in his own hands.

"*Hola*, Lilibeth." He kissed her on the lips, as though family. He tousled Antony's hair, then kissed his plump cheek noisily. "Antony is beautiful. Like you." He looked over to capture Marisel's gaze. "Like his *abuela*."

He left Lili still holding the door and walked to Marisel. He stood before her and spoke quietly. "Are you ashamed to be my woman?"

Her hand muffled a small moan. She shook her head and tears glimmered in her eyes. She took her hand from her mouth and placed it on his chest. She straightened a little, then stepped close to him. "No, Emilio. *Lo siento.* I am not ashamed. I am proud."

He circled his arms around her. "*Esta bien.*" He put his lips on hers and took, more than he should have with her daughter standing there watching, less than he wanted.

When he let her go, she smiled shakily and stepped back, her cheeks pink. "Lili, set another place. Sit, if you like, Emilio." She gestured to the couch in front of the television. "We'll have dinner soon."

He looked at the television. It was off now and there was certain to be nothing more interesting to watch than the two women in whose presence he found himself.

"*Gracias*, no. I'll take Antony while you finish in the kitchen."

He walked back to Lilibeth and took the baby in his arms. "I helped with my nephew."

Lilibeth gave him a skeptical look but agreed, obviously willing to be amused at his expense. "*Si.*"

The women exchanged glances, then walked to the kitchen. Emilio followed them, more or less comfortable with the baby in his arms, entirely comfortable watching the sway of feminine hips before him.

A griddle was hot, dusted with flour for tortillas. A pot of beans simmered and some kind of meat in chili sauce cooled on a back burner. The women busied themselves, glancing at him a bit nervously. He went to a fruit bowl, snagged a banana, then sat at the table to share with Antony. And teach the boy about girl watching.

They ate together, chatting a bit, entertained by Antony in his highchair. When they finished the meal, they each took part in clean up. The last dish put away, Lilibeth turned to her mother.

"Mama?"

Marisel looked up at Emilio. "She wanted to go out tonight. She has a date. I said I would watch the baby."

"You know the boy, Mari?"

"*Si*. Josef. He's a good boy."

"Is he coming here for you, Lilibeth?"

Lilibeth looked from him to her mother but got no help there. She answered grudgingly. "No. I'm meeting him at my friend Serena's house."

"Ask him, please, to come here next time. I'd like to meet Josef. Be sure to tell him I'm a cop. And I'll want to know his last name."

She looked mutinous, but conceded. "*Si*. It's Garcia." She turned to her mother and kissed her, saying goodnight, then did the same with Antony. She started to circle around Emilio.

He wasn't done. He stopped her with a hand on her arm. "What time will you be home, Lili?"

She paused a beat, frowning, tapping her foot, then gave up. "Midnight."

"Okay." Emilio leaned down and kissed her, held her another minute. "Have fun. Be good."

He could see her stop herself from rolling her eyes.

"*Si. Buenos nochas.*"

He let her go and she left the kitchen. He looked at Marisel, and she returned his gaze steadily.

After a moment, she smiled. "Are you waiting for me to object to how you were with her?"

"I was wondering."

She came to him and kissed him, hand stroking his cheek. "I do not object. But I wonder, how do you feel about spending the evening with a baby?"

He picked up Antony from the highchair, then walked with his arm around Marisel to the living room. "I do not object. He'll go to sleep sometime, *si*?"

She laughed at his leer. When she settled on the couch, he handed down Antony and then sat close to her.

"*Maybe* he will sleep. He's not famous for it." She looked at him when he put his arm around her and began to nuzzle. "I don't want you to stay the night here, Emilio, not with Lili coming home."

He wanted to kiss her senseless, touch her everywhere, bury himself inside her. Instead, he stroked his hand over Antony's curls, sending him a silent sleep inducement. "Would it be different, Mari, if you promised to marry me?"

Her breath trembled on a sigh. "*Si.*"

He looked deep into her eyes, letting her know how much he wanted her. "*Si*, it would be different? Or, *si*, you will marry me?"

"*Si*, both, Emilio."

He gave her a lingering kiss, distracted only slightly by wet, pudgy fingers grasping at his cheek. "You make me very happy, Marisel."

"You make me happy, Emilio."

That settled, he reached for the remote, then sank back into the couch with Marisel and the baby snug in his arms. He found that he watched them more than the TV, exchanging kisses, some warm, some just drooly wet, until Antony finally drifted off against his grandmother's chest.

"You look good with a baby in your arms, Mari."

She looked up, searched his eyes.

"I'd like to see you with a baby at your breast, *querida*.

That would be a sight."

"Emilio, I don't know. I am old."

He laughed, stroking the soft, smooth skin of her cheek. "You're not old." He held her as she tried to turn her face from him. "If it were possible, if it were safe. And if you want to be a mother again, it's something I would like very much."

Tears filled her eyes, falling down her cheeks when she blinked. He put his lips to them to kiss them away.

"I would like it very much, too."

His voice was husky when he spoke. "*Querida*. Put the baby in his crib."

Later, he was in her bed. Marisel had lit candles, filling the room with soft light and seductive scent. He'd touched her everywhere and now was buried deep inside her. He hadn't used a condom. The feel of her, the heat and wetness, without that barrier, was driving him fast over the brink.

But there was one thing he needed to say. He grasped at the frayed edges of his control, thrust once more as far as he could go into her, and held himself there.

She was far gone into it, too, breathing hard and straining against him. It took a few moments for her to realize he'd stopped moving. When she did, she opened her eyes to him.

He held her face, rubbed his thumb hard over her moist, swollen lips. "Mari." He struggled to hold on as the climax threatened to overtake them both. "You are young now and beautiful. But I will still love you when you are old and wrinkled."

She gave him a slow, woman's smile, then touched her tongue to his thumb.

With that visual, desire broke free of control. He grasped at her, and she at him, fingers digging in for purchase. Muscles tensed, bodies arched, they took each other, hard and long, over the edge.

Cooper spent a long time in a hot shower after his workout at the police gym. His bruises from the game were fading, but he still felt a few of them. He made a mental note to remember next November that he was too old for this.

After he dressed, he stowed his gear back in his locker, then grabbed for his keys. He was about to slip them into his jacket pocket when he noticed he'd lost his GTO key fob. He paused for a moment, reminiscing. It had been a gift from his ex-fiancée. For a short time, it had given him hope that she understood him at least a little. Now it was gone, with a past that was gone, and he didn't have to grasp at straws to have hope for his future.

When he pulled into his drive, he decided his future looked damn good. Sylvia's car was there and lights were on in the house. She'd used the key he'd given her.

Smiling, he wondered if she cooked.

CHAPTER THIRTEEN

Thanksgiving week was quiet. Cooper and Emilio spent the days consulting with Sullivan, tying together the strands that would form a web securely around Parsons.

Sylvia swore the gangs had made no contact with her; nonetheless, the street was quiet around Tynie's Place. Cooper didn't know what to make of it, but they all breathed a little easier. Still, he wasn't ready to acknowledge the superior looks Sylvia occasionally gave him, or to reduce the level of protection he was providing at the birth center.

Thus he dozed on Sylvia's office couch Wednesday evening while she took care of a woman in labor upstairs. When he woke, shortly after midnight, he was pretty sure he remembered that she'd come to him. He was seduced out of sleep with her hands on him, and then her mouth. When he was hard and straining, she lifted herself over him and sank down, taking him in deep. He reached for her, greedy to touch. She tore her shirt off and opened her bra, her breasts jutting proudly, bouncing firmly as she rode him.

He filled his hands with them, squeezing, rubbing at her nipples. She hummed her pleasure, and he arched into her, opening her legs wider, pressing himself up into her heat.

They moved together, teasing, reaching higher. He wanted more of her, but he didn't want to let go, either. He spoke brusquely. "Push your tits together for me."

Without question, she complied. He grabbed at her, grasping both nipples between the fingers of one hand, strumming his thumb back and forth across them.

He slipped his free hand down, knuckling her where their bodies joined. She groaned and moved against him. "Now," he said, compelling her. "Faster. Now."

She moved on him until she spasmed, her body arching wildly. He thrust a few more times, pumping into her until he, too, was spent.

She rested against him for a few minutes, then gathered her discarded clothes and went into the bathroom. He didn't remember when she left the office.

He was pretty sure it had all happened. If it was a dream, he'd have awakened with a hell of a boner, not the useless, flaccid thing she'd left him with.

He grinned for a minute, savoring the memory. Then he remembered the night's work ahead and his smile faded. He rolled off the couch, fastened his jeans, and reached for his boots.

✦ ✳ ✦

C.J. Lawton was in the smoke-filled back room of a night-club off Hudson Avenue. Cooper had tracked him through a series of his homeboys, employing harassment techniques that skirted a fine line just inside of legality.

Revelers in the club seemed to pay him no mind as he traversed the main room, but Cooper knew hostile eyes watched from behind tinted glass. He moved to the back room, coming chest to chest with the goon at the door. After neither of them blinked for a while, Cooper spoke.

"My name's Billings. I'm here to see C.J."

The guy still didn't flinch.

"Trust me, he wants to see me."

The brute stuck a hard finger in his chest to convince him to stay put while he stepped through the door, closing it behind him. In a moment, he opened it and beckoned Cooper in.

Lawton sat at a table spread with cards, poker chips, and shot glasses. A young woman was perched on his lap, her skirt hiked up to her hips and one lush breast exposed. Clearly, he had something to play with if the cards lost their attraction.

He leaned back in his chair and met Cooper's gaze. He put his cards on the table, then fondled the woman's breast, tweaking her nipple. The woman tongued his ear and spread her knees open. The other three guys at the table looked between that action and Cooper, smirks on their faces.

Cooper perused each of them. They were glassy-eyed, stoned. They'd all have a handgun tucked somewhere, he knew, but they'd be slow to move. Only the goon was alert, but he was too muscle bound to move fast. Still, he stepped enough to the side to keep him in his line of vision.

C.J.'s eyes followed him, sharp, his cocky nonchalance a pretense only. "What you want, cop?"

"Parsons told me to hook up with you. He's bringing me in."

The dark eyes flickered, then the façade was back. "Funny. The preacher told me we was taking you out. Bringing in. Taking out. Hard to confuse those two."

Cooper nodded once. "We came to terms. Mutually beneficial."

"Don't see what that has to do with me."

"I'm taking over shipping. You and I are going to go over this end of it. Next week, I'm in Baltimore, picking up that end."

"This end be my job."

"It's still your job. It's just that I'm your boss, now."

"You ain't my boss 'til I hear it from Parsons."

"You've got a phone. Call him."

C.J. shook his head. "I ain't calling him now. He with his pussy."

Cooper knew that. He'd followed Parsons to East Avenue Towers, where the man kept his favorite mistress. His Mercedes sedan was in the covered lot, would be there for hours. His driver sat inside, entertaining himself with porn videos running on a laptop. The driver wasn't local—he looked like a pro, probably assigned by Parsons's connection in Baltimore. A little protection for his assets. "Fine. Check it out with him tomorrow."

He took his business card from a pocket and placed it on the table. "Call me on Friday. We'll get to work."

He walked out. Back in his car, he drove automatically, putting some distance between himself and the club. He circled the Cobb's Hill reservoir then parked where he could watch the city lights. His fingers found the silver cross that dangled on his chest. He rubbed it over his lips, tapped it against his teeth.

Parsons was the man behind the gang takeover. Parsons was bringing drugs in through Baltimore. Eyes closed, drifting, Cooper heard the pop of automatic gunfire, saw the flash. Remembering, he caught the scent of gun smoke and the smells of the harbor. Parsons had been there that night at the Baltimore harbor. He was the one they'd been after. He was responsible for the deaths of two cops. He was responsible for Teddy Washington's injury.

Cooper took the cross and tucked it back into his shirt. C.J. hadn't bothered to lie about Parsons. That meant he hadn't lied about something else. They'd already decided to take him out.

Thanksgiving tradition mandated that all the O'Dades return to Russ and Marge's old Browncroft colonial, large enough to still hold them all. Katherine Huston and Travis Sullivan were present, as well as Sylvia and Cooper. Emilio and Marisel were invited also, and came with little Antony.

It was a boisterous, friendly crowd. The women gathered mostly in the large kitchen, delicious smells and entirely feminine laughter emanating from there. After a trip in for a beer refill, Brendan reported that they'd killed their sixth bottle of wine and were getting a little rowdy.

Cooper knew he was blushing when he returned to the male safety of the living room from his last—he swore it would be—foray into the kitchen. He placed a bowl on the card table where a serious game of poker was underway. He'd dropped forty bucks before he had the convenient craving for more dip. He was sure the O'Dade boys cheated, he just hadn't caught them at it yet.

He socked Jed on the arm. "You should control your wife a little better, dude."

"She groping the goods, again?"

"Um-hmm. And her eyes got real big like she'd never experienced anything like it before."

Jed's brothers snickered. Even Russ, who was in a supposedly serious conversation with Emilio and Travis, snorted.

Jed gave Cooper a look. "I ain't been hearing no complaints."

"Yeah, well, you know what they say. It's hard to keep 'em down on the farm..."

Jed was in the process of saying, "Stuff it, Billings," when there was a loud harrumph at the door. Sylvia stood there, leaning with arms across her chest.

"What was that about a farm, Coop?"

"Turkey farms, Sylvia. We were talking about the economic impact of Thanksgiving traditions on local farmers."

Brendan let out a huge belch. "Yeah, and beer stores."
David lifted his longneck. "Beer stores. Good one."
Sylvia sniffed while the guys clinked bottles. "We're all
busy in the kitchen..."

"Not too busy to spare time for a little sexual harassment," Cooper said, but mostly under his breath.

Sylvia cleared her throat loudly and continued. "We wondered if any of you extremely hard-working men were keeping an eye on the kids."

"I checked on them a few minutes ago," Russ said. His
sons and Cooper toasted him in a show of male solidarity.
"Most of them were busy with *Mario Speedway*. A couple of
the little ones were making a mess with Play-Doh. They're
okay."

"You can tell Madalyn I got Jesse down for his nap," David added. "And Bren took care of Sam. They're both up on
Mom's bed."

"Yeah," said Brendan, though it might have been another
belch.

"Good," said Sylvia, a bit deflated. "We eat in about twenty minutes." She gave them all another look, shaking her
head. "This is such a guy holiday. You sit around, drink beer,
and get fed."

A chorus of cheery agreement sounded. "And football.
Don't forget football."

She rolled her eyes and was gone.

Emilio rested his arm along the back of Marisel's chair,
toying with a strand of her hair. He considered whether he
could discreetly loosen his belt, as he was sure he'd seen
Russ and Travis do, but he resisted the urge.

The family had happily spent an hour devouring the remarkable feast. They'd brought the children around them—
onto laps or tucked underarm, for grace and thanks. Then
they'd sent them all off with a full plate to the junior table in
the den.

Despite avid attention to the food, conversation was ani-
mated. The brothers entertained with apparently well-
embellished stories of past holidays, the finer points of which

were often contested. Jed had Tessie blushing as he recount-ed the Christmas Eve when their second son had been born on the way to the hospital—she hadn't wanted to cause a fuss during the family gift exchange.

Emilio noticed that the men began exchanging glances as the conversation dwindled. After a bit of that, Russ stood up. He patted his belly and looked around the table. "Ladies, you outdid yourselves. I won't eat again for a week."

The women at the table who were in the know gave him a grin. Katherine spoke. "I guess that leaves more pumpkin pie for the rest of us."

Russ objected quickly. "Oh, no. I saved room. I'll just give it an hour or two, in order to clear the palate. I'm sure it deserves my full appreciation."

That brought a round of cheers and jeers, pretty much along gender lines.

Russ picked up his plate and utensils. "In the meantime, I think someone ought to check on the kids. They've been a bit too quiet in there for my comfort."

He walked to the other end of the table and gave Marge a smooch. "It was lovely, darlin'. As usual."

Marge patted his butt as he headed to the kitchen and Russ's subsequent little hop had his sons snickering.

One by one, the other men picked up their plates, kissed their wives—some spent a little minute at it—mentioned a concern about the children, and left the table.

Finally, only Cooper and Emilio were left. Cooper was faster. He shrugged, took his plate, kissed Sylvia, and left.

Emilio looked around the table, meeting several pairs of blue eyes. A bit sheepishly, he got to his feet. "Thank you all for a lovely dinner. It was exquisite. I guess I'll go, uh, check on the kids."

He started to pick up his plate, but stopped as Marisel signaled him. He floundered, confused for a minute, until she whispered to him.

He left his dishes, but took Antony up from his highchair. He did not forget to kiss Marisel. Baby in his arms, he fol-lowed the sounds of cheering and argument to the den.

The men were all there, in easy chairs, on the couch, stretched out on the floor. Many had kids on their laps or crawling over them. All had their attention on the big screen TV.

Brendan looked up between plays. "Emilio, Tonio. Come on in." He nudged over to make room on the couch. "Football."

It was late—and the pumpkin pie was gone—when the parents began to bundle sleepy children into coats and mittens. Avoiding the mass confusion, Cooper backed Sylvia into a corner of the kitchen. He had every intention of making out with her and wrangling an invitation to her place for the night.

She giggled, though her breath caught just a little, as he went for the—apparently it was tradition—butt pat. He nuzzled her along her neck, slid his tongue up behind her ear.

"You need to sleep tonight. I can help you out with that."

She laughed, but he knew she had to work at it—her body was arching up against his.

"You want to help me sleep?"

He squeezed where he'd left his hand, sliding a little deeper. He liked the little hum she gave him. "You know I've got the technique."

She lifted her arms around him and he knew he had her. He put his mouth on hers, exploring gently as he savored his blessings.

She smiled through the kiss. "So you do."

"I love you. I love your family. I've never enjoyed Thanksgiving before, never had even a moderately good time. This was great. Thanks for bringing me."

"You're welcome. Guess you made things up with the boys, eh?"

"They're all right. One thing, though—" He let his hands explore a little more, one finding its way up under her sweater, one slipping inside her slacks. "Except for you, this family has nothing but boys. We get to have a girl, don't we?"

Sylvia giggled again, having some difficulty at it with his tongue chasing after hers. "I don't know. We may have to work at it, try a few times."

He sank into her, then pulled back, reminding himself that they were in her aunt's kitchen. "I'm willing to do my part. But I think we should get started. Tonight."

"Um. I thought we were putting me to sleep tonight."

"Multitasking."

She laughed again, and then he sighed as his pager went

off. A moment later, from the living room, he heard Emilio's.

He held Sylvia close against him for another minute, then let her go. "Sounds like I'll be busy tonight. Have Travis take you home, please. I don't want you to drive yourself."

She looked up at him, bound to object. He shushed her with a kiss. "You haven't slept. Please. I'll bring you back for your car tomorrow."

He felt a small victory when she relented. "Thanks, baby." He kissed her again, lingered over it. "I love you."

She grabbed at his hand as he started to leave. "Be careful."

He saw the real fear in her eyes and stepped back to her, holding her face up to his. "I will. You know I will."

He watched her eyes until she nodded. He kissed her again and left her.

In the living room, Emilio had his coat on and was closing up his cell phone. "You can drive?"

At Cooper's nod, he handed his car keys to Marisel. "You'll be okay?"

Marisel gave him her assurance, and Jed said they'd help her load up Antony.

Travis Sullivan stood next to Katherine, helping her with her coat. Cooper caught his eye. "I asked Sylvie to catch a ride home with you. She hasn't slept."

Sullivan nodded. "I'll see to it. Give me a call later. I've got my cell."

Cooper understood the message. The lieutenant might not be spending the night in his own house. He was another man who was hoping to get lucky.

Cooper drove as Emilio took directions. Someone out on this cold night had found a dead body in an empty lot off Thurston, on the border between Latin Kings and Plymouth Rocks territory. After he finished that call, Emilio checked in with the man they had at Tynie's Place, to let him know Marisel was on her way.

The rain that had pelted down all day had now turned to ice; already the trees were coated. The roads had a thin sheen of ice, too. By the streetlights, Cooper watched the freezing rain slash down. His mind flashed to the night a few weeks ago when he'd first seen Sylvia. He remembered the perception of strangeness, that sense of the extraordinary he'd felt then.

He felt it again now and suppressed a shudder. He kept his attention on the road until his cell phone rang.

"Billings."

"Coop. It's Jackson."

"Yeah?"

"I'm at the scene. You on your way?"

"Yeah. I've got Emilio. We're just about there."

"Pull over, man."

He glanced over at Emilio and pulled the car to the curb. "What is it?"

"The stiff is C.J. Lawton. Somebody beat the crap out of him. He's got your card in his pocket, and there's a GTO key fob on the ground."

"Shit." Considering, he reached and turned off the ignition.

"There's more."

"Bet you saved the good news for last."

"Somebody called the Chief. He's here, got steam coming out of his ears. A news crew, too."

"Hell." He paused, fully aware of the chance Jackson was taking with this call. "Thanks, man. I owe you."

"Watch your back."

Cooper closed his phone and told Emilio the tale. They sat in the dark, close enough to the scene to see the flash of lights and to watch another news van pull up.

Emilio gazed out the window. "How'd they get your stuff?"

"I gave him my card myself. It'll have my prints. I noticed my key fob was missing after I worked out at the gym last week."

"They broke into your locker."

Cooper rubbed at the back of his neck. "I'm guessing."

"They've got somebody on the force."

Cooper nodded.

"What else was in your locker?"

"What else do they need?"

"You have a hairbrush in there?"

"Yeah. Shit. So they'll find one of my hairs on the body, have a DNA match."

"We always knew he was smart." Emilio's face was grim. "So he thinks he's taken care of you. What else does he want?"

"Shit. Sylvia."

Sylvia leaned over the back of the seat and kissed her mother and godfather goodnight. She went up the steps to her house, let herself in, and, with a thought to Cooper, carefully locked the door behind her. By the light of the living room—also one of Cooper's safety lessons, never leave the house dark—she hung her coat in the closet. Then she did a yoga stretch, working at the fatigue in her neck and shoulders.

She was smiling when she stepped toward the living room. She'd had a wonderful day, starting with a fine birth in the early morning hours and ending with a make-out session with Cooper in Marge's kitchen after a lovely family dinner. Not to mention mind-numbing sex on her office couch in the middle of the night.

She nearly hugged herself in joy. She loved Cooper. She was not going to fight it. She would learn how to live with the risks inherent in his job. She would be grateful for their love. They'd conceive and raise their children in that love. And she would pray every day that they'd both be old and gray when they died.

She looked forward to falling into bed. She would sleep, even without Cooper's help. Then she swung around the corner into the living room. Her smile vanished, along with that feeling of hopefulness.

"She's in trouble." Cooper knew it, as he'd known she was the one for him that other night of freezing rain.

He turned the key in the ignition and pulled a U-turn, wrenching down on the panic that made him want to peel out, tires squealing. They didn't need the attention of either the cops or the news crews at the scene. A few blocks away, he punched the accelerator and sped in the direction of Sylvia's place.

Simultaneously, Emilio and he dialed numbers into their cell phones. The uniform on the job at the birth center reported that Marisel hadn't arrived yet. Emilio instructed the man to keep his eyes open and to call when she showed.

Cooper got the lieutenant.

"Sullivan."

"It's Coop. Are you on speaker?"

There was no answer for a moment, and Cooper waited impatiently, knowing that Travis would carefully pull over before he lifted the phone.

"No. What's up?"

"Do you still have Sylvie with you?"

There was a short pause, and Cooper was aware that Katherine Huston occupied the seat next to the Lieutenant.

"No."

Cooper cursed and didn't hold back about it. "Lawton's dead." He hesitated, considering whether there was any way to protect Sullivan in the event this all went to hell. The man had already stood up to the chief for him, gone out on a limb. Then he shrugged, realizing that Travis wouldn't thank him for the thought—he'd been managing department politics since Cooper was in diapers. Besides, it was Sylvia at stake.

"He was beaten to death. Personal items belonging to me are at the scene."

"A set-up."

"Yeah."

"Parsons?"

"Yeah. I think he's gone for Sylvia."

"Wouldn't he look for her at..."

Cooper completed the thought for him. "At Tynie's Place? Yeah, you'd think. But I'm pretty sure he's already got her."

"Where are you?"

"On Goodman. I've got Emilio. We'll be at her house in five minutes."

"You going in with sirens?"

"No."

"You want blue and whites?"

"No."

"What can I do?"

"Katherine's not stupid. I imagine she's in a panic by now. Take care of her. We'll get Sylvia."

"Good luck."

"Yeah."

Five blocks from Sylvia's house, Travis Sullivan set the phone back in its cradle. He turned to the woman in the seat beside him.

"I'd like you to take the car and drive yourself home."

"No."

"Katherine—"

"Sylvia's in trouble, isn't she?"

"We're not certain—"

"And you're going to help her."

He sighed, put his hands on her shoulders to pull her close. "Yes."

"Okay." She kissed him, hard, on the lips. "Be careful."

"I will." He kissed her back, softly. "Stay here. Keep the doors locked. I'll call you on that phone when I can."

He popped the trunk and got out. After a couple minutes, he slammed the trunk closed, met Katherine's gaze through the rear window, and walked away.

Noah Parsons. Sylvia recognized him as he rose from her couch and for a single, bizarre moment, she almost cried out in relief. But of course, that was wrong. It didn't matter that she knew who the intruder was. That fact only made matters worse.

He spoke her name in his rich, honeyed voice. He walked toward her and she caught the scent of his cologne. Before she could stir herself to turn and run, he was upon her.

Her breath caught in fear as his left hand circled around her throat. She tried to step away, and he followed until her back was pressed against the wall. He kept his right hand in the pocket of his long leather coat.

He wedged his thumb against her chin until she lifted her eyes to his.

"I've been waiting for you, Sylvia. I don't like to have to wait for a woman."

She understood he meant more than just this night. "I'm

not going to be with you. I'm going to marry Cooper."

"Billings is under arrest. I imagine he'll die in prison with a shiv in his neck. In fact, I'll make sure of it."

She kept quiet, dreading to hear what this man had done. He caressed with his thumb, and she fought to still a shudder.

"You doubt me, don't you? Soon you'll learn better. Your boyfriend killed C.J. Lawton in a jealous rage, beat him to a bloody pulp. C.J. dared to touch you, put his hand on your breast."

She closed her eyes, stopping herself from shaking her head in denial.

He leaned closer to her, nearly touching. "Of course, I understand his reaction. I'd do the same, now that you're mine."

Anger quelled some of the fear. She put a hand against his chest. "I'm not yours. I never will be."

He pulled a handgun out of his pocket. He stroked with it down her neck to the vee of her sweater, followed that to her breast. "You will be. One way." He slipped the barrel of the gun into her bra and rubbed it against her nipple. "Or another."

Sylvia pressed back against the wall and spit in his face. He brought his gun hand out of her sweater to wipe at his face, his eyes lighting obscenely. He pushed his knee between her legs, hard. "I enjoy it rough, but I do like to be comfortable."

He dragged her around the corner and shoved her toward the stairs. "Go upstairs."

She caught herself from stumbling. She remembered the night she'd met with the Rocks, when Cooper had come to her in such anger. His words swirled in her brain. *Don't go with him easily. He'll have trouble controlling you and his weapon, too.*

She dug her feet in. If he wanted her upstairs, he'd have to carry her. He pushed again, trying to force her. They nearly toppled over when they reached the steps, and she refused to lift her feet.

"Go, goddammit!"

"No."

He swore again and turned her. He slammed her into the wall beside the stairs. He stood with one arm extended, bracing her against it. The other held his gun, the black luster threatening. Sylvia looked from it into his eyes. With another curse, he brought the gun crashing into her temple.

Cooper pulled the GTO into an open space a couple blocks from Sylvia's house. He and Emilio got out and met at the trunk. With a flashlight, they scanned the items stored there.

Emilio nodded his head in approval. "What are the chances he came alone?"

Cooper considered. "I don't know. He expects I'm downtown defending myself against a murder charge. Probably thinks you're there, too. That would leave him clear to make a play for Sylvia."

"Probably doesn't think he needs help for that."

"Nope. But he doesn't take chances. Takes his bodyguard with him when he screws his mistress."

Emilio snorted. "Gotta figure he'd be more cautious tonight. Sylvia's tough, in her way."

Cooper took a breath, willing his heart and his voice to be steady. "Yeah."

Emilio turned and put a hand on his shoulder. "She is, you know. Whatever happens, she'll survive it."

Cooper nodded but couldn't make eye contact. He reached into the trunk for supplies.

Emilio did the same. "So we should assume he brought protection."

Cooper agreed. "Probably one in front, one in back."

"Pros, you think, or a couple of his homeboys?"

Cooper pulled a roll of duct tape from a duffle. He tore off several strips, folded over an inch at one end, and stuck them across his chest. He met Emilio's eyes when he handed the roll over.

"Don't know. Maybe both. His driver looked imported, probably pro. He might have homies, too. Be safer for us to count on them being pros."

Emilio nodded as he made his own strips. He dug through the bag, too, brought out a couple plastic ratchet cuffs and stuffed them in a pocket.

"Sylvie's house has a walk-out basement." Cooper slipped into his shoulder holster. "Give me ten minutes to make my way around the back. You find whoever he's got in front, then come in after me."

"We're not going to know how many men he's got."

"Nope."

"We should get back-up." Emilio bent to strap a knife to his leg.

"As soon as we have Sylvia safe." He took two flashlights from the bag, pocketed one and gave the other to his partner. They crouched down in the shadow of the car. At the curb, they pulled up tufts of old brown grass and dug into the mud underneath. They smeared their hands and faces with it, cursing the fact that they'd worn semi-dress clothes.

Having done what they could to camouflage themselves, they stood and faced each other.

Emilio put a heavy hand on Cooper's shoulder. "We can nail Parsons on conspiracy, and we have him on the drugs, too. He's going to spend a long time behind bars."

Cooper read his partner's eyes. "I won't kill him. Unless it comes to it."

Reassured, Emilio nodded. "Let's go, then."

Cooper stopped him. "The last time I went after this guy, my partner nearly died. Watch your back."

Emilio grinned and slugged his shoulder. "Eyes in the back of my head, partner."

✦ ✖ ✦

Sylvia rolled to her side and groaned as she lifted a hand to her aching head. She pushed herself upright, then waited for the room to stop spinning. She was on her living room sofa. Parsons sat on the edge of the coffee table facing her, the gun in his hand resting carelessly on his thigh. With lewd interest, he watched her wake.

She brushed hair away from her face and looked back at him. "Why are you doing this?"

Parsons shrugged. "You piqued my interest, that day at the birth center when you refused me. You pretended you didn't even know I was coming on to you."

Gently, aware of throbbing pain, she shook her head. "How could that mean anything to you? You can have almost any woman you want."

"I want you. I've spent a lot of years arranging my life so I can have anything I want."

Anything. That was how Parsons saw her: a plaything, to amuse him and stroke his ego. Still, his behavior seemed over the top. "That's why you set up Cooper? Just so you could have me?"

"Don't flatter yourself. Though I will say you raised my ire, kissing him in front of Tynie's Place, practically letting him screw you there in the street."

The thought of him watching that day sent a chill through her. She pulled herself up to sit.

Parsons leaned forward, keeping the gun aimed at her. "Billings has made some unfortunate connections to our mutual past. He's a threat to the life I've established here."

"And so you killed C.J.? To frame Cooper?"

"Oh, C.J. was dead anyway. He did put his hands on you, remember? Do you know he defended you? Wanted to help you keep your precious birth center safe?"

She lifted her head to look up at him, then ducked it again as the movement set the room twirling. He reached forward and tilted her head back up, not gently, with the gun in his hand.

She struggled to push his arm away, but he held tight, moved his mouth close to hers. "I understand Tynie's Place is important to you. I'm sure that we can come to an agreeable arrangement."

Her eyes closed as his mouth descended.

Down the block, Cooper stole into a back yard. He hoped like hell the crappy weather had kept all the neighborhood dogs inside.

He dropped over a fence into the yard next door to Sylvia's. He crossed it on his belly, staying in the shadows of bushes and trees. A picket fence separated the yards. He stopped there and peered through the slats of the fence.

He watched for several minutes. There was no movement, no sound. Silently, he cursed. He had to figure Parsons had brought in professionals. Punks from the gang would never have the patience to remain still and silent.

Then, from beside the rhododendron at Sylvia's back door, he saw the flare of a lighter and, after a moment, caught a waft of marijuana smoke. Grimly, he smiled. Not a pro, after all.

He searched the area around him, found a little ceramic frog of the sort that always made him roll his eyes. No accounting for taste in garden décor. He took it in his left hand and drew his gun from its holster with his right. He followed the fence until he melded with the shadows of the two houses.

His position as protected as it could be, he hiked himself over the fence, the soft mulch of Sylvia's flowerbeds quiet under his feet. He crept along the foundation until he neared the rhododendron. Then, figuring the frog would never serve a greater purpose, he tossed it up and over. It crashed gratifyingly on the small stone patio.

Reactions slow either from the drug or just naturally dull wits, the man beside the shrub turned belatedly toward the clatter. Cooper stepped up behind and with his gun nudged him firmly between the shoulder blades.

"To your knees. Don't make a sound."

The guy let out a whiney curse—Cooper figured he was mad he'd ruined a good high—then complied. He'd obviously been through the drill before as he placed his hands behind his back without instruction.

Cooper cuffed him, then pulled him to his feet. He pushed him in the direction of a small maple tree. "How many guys does Parsons have out front?"

When all he got was a crude instruction about unlikely sexual functions, Cooper gave the kid a little tap with the butt of his Colt. Once he'd gotten his attention, the answer was more to the point, though not any friendlier. "One, asshole."

"Lie down there, put your feet on either side of the tree."

"Ah, man."

He couldn't blame the kid for objecting. The leaves hadn't been raked and were wet and slimy. Cooper figured they provided a happy home for whole families of slugs. Obviously, he was going to have to help Sylvia with fall clean up.

He lifted a brow, and the kid bowed to the inevitable, though not gracefully. Cooper used ratchet cuffs to secure his ankles together on the far side of the tree trunk. Then he slapped a couple straps of duct tape across his mouth to form a gag. He'd be quiet, and he'd stay put. He wouldn't be very comfortable, but Cooper figured he could sue later.

He tapped his Colt through the lower pane of the back door, then reached in to turn the simple lock. Shaking his head at Sylvia's inadequate security measures, he slipped quietly into the basement.

Parsons jerked back from Sylvia when the crashing sound came from the back yard. Standing abruptly, he pulled her to her feet. He backed up against the fireplace and held her tightly in front of him, gun against her temple. Agitation in his voice, he called out. "Vincent! Get in here!"

The front door opened and in a moment Sylvia saw Emilio. His hands were clasped at the back of his neck as a man holding a gun pushed him into the room. His eyes scanned the room quickly and came back to rest gently on hers.

He spoke softly, as if they were alone. "He hurt you, Sylvia?"

In her head, she heard the consequence of that. *He would pay.* She trembled, afraid now for both of them. "I'm okay."

The man behind Emilio shoved him into a chair. He looked around, then pulled the cord from a table lamp, smashing it to the floor. With the cord, he secured Emilio's hands behind the chair.

Then he rose up to his full height and turned a menacing gaze on Parsons. He was a big man, the ebony skin of his shaved head gleaming. His body was that of a muscle builder, incongruously fit into an expertly tailored silk suit. It did nothing to diminish the air of danger about him.

Sylvia felt the tremor in the gun that pressed at her temple and heard it in Parsons's voice. "Vincent, why'd you bring him in here?"

Vincent bristled. "He's a cop. What'd you want me to do with him? Man, you said you'd taken care of the cop."

"He meant me."

Cooper held his gun down at his side and stepped through the hall to the living room. He met Emilio's eyes first. "How many?"

"I found one, missed this one. Haven't seen anyone else." He jerked his head toward the man behind him. "This guy's a pro. Take him out first. Parsons is losing it."

"No big. He's just the driver. Must have gotten tired of jerking off in the Mercedes."

Cooper fielded Vincent's offended look and grinned evilly back at him. He was the muscle from Baltimore, and professional enough to know when a situation was going all to hell.

He turned his attention to the far side of the room. The moment he'd understood that Sylvia had been taken, Cooper had encased his heart in ice. It was a hard but fragile armor, nearly cracking now at the sight of Sylvia held captive, gun at her head. He felt a draft of cool air from the door; it was only that thing that let him breathe.

Parsons's face glistened with sweat. His hand trembled so the gun at Sylvia's temple shook. "You should've stayed away, Billings."

"You should've kept your hands off my woman." Finally, he met Sylvia's eyes. He noted the bruise, worked at shoring up the ice. "You okay, baby?"

She nodded, her eyes held to his.

"The lock on your back door's no damn good, honey. I'll work on it for you tomorrow."

He saw trust overcome the fear in her eyes. She gave him a small smile. "Okay."

"Your yard is a mess, too. Do you not own a rake?"

Her smile strengthened a bit. "I'll get one."

He felt better at her response, but he didn't let it show in his face. "You don't look so good, baby. Everything's going to be all right. Just take some deep breaths. Parsons, she needs to sit down."

Vincent lifted his gun to point it at Cooper. "Shut the hell up. Parsons, what do you want me to do?"

Cooper signaled and Sylvia got the message. Her knees gave way and she sank toward the floor. Parsons bobbled the gun as he tried to hold her, his chest now unprotected. At the same moment, Travis Sullivan appeared at Cooper's side. Emilio kicked back his chair, effectively removing Vincent's cover.

Three men fired as one. Two shots from Cooper's gun hit Parsons in the chest. Sullivan and Vincent exchanged shots. Both men slammed back and fell to the floor.

Emilio surged to his feet, knocking aside the chair, his hands still bound behind his back. He kicked the gun away from Vincent. Dragging the broken lamp, he went to Parsons and did the same. It was an unnecessary precaution; neither man was breathing.

Sylvia rolled away from Parsons. "Travis!" She ran to his side. Cooper was already there, kneeling over the older man.

Sullivan's eyes were open. His breath was shallow but steady. Cooper tore at his shirt, opened it up so they could see the vest.

Cooper smiled as Sullivan began to cuss about being kicked by a mule. He clapped the lieutenant on the shoulder. "Good man." He reached across and touched Sylvia, feeling his heart beating again, ice gone. "Good girl."

Sylvia smiled and squeezed his hand. She grabbed a couple couch pillows and propped them under Sullivan's head. Cooper took a knife to the electric cord that bound Emilio, then dialed 911 for ambulance and police assistance.

Travis cursed some more. "One of those guys need an ambulance? Because I don't."

Cooper smirked just a little. "Procedure, Lieutenant. You wouldn't want us to go against procedure, would you?"

He swore again, then looked at Sylvia. "Dial my cell. Your mother's in my car, a few blocks from here."

Soon the house was full. Travis rested on the couch, with Katherine clucking over him. Half the police department seemed to be there, taking care of Parsons and Vincent, collecting the man Cooper had cuffed to the tree and another Emilio had left bound out front.

In the end, Sullivan agreed to go by car to be checked out in the hospital. Cooper drove, Sylvia at his side, Travis and Katherine in the back. He left the couple at the hospital warning the lieutenant to watch out for a patient care tech by the name of Venda.

He drove Sylvia to his house, tucked her into his bed. He held her until she slept, then left to join Emilio. There were hours of paperwork to do, details to be finessed, an angry chief to be mollified.

And a bad cop to be found.

It was light when Cooper crawled back into bed with Sylvia. Bright, in fact, with the sun lighting up the ice-coated trees like a fairyland.

She turned to him in a most gratifying way, still mostly asleep, but taking him into the warmth of her arms.

"You okay, baby?"

A smile touched her lips. "I'm fine, stud muffin."

"You going to call me that every time I call you baby?"

"I might."

He kissed the smile away. "Guess I can live with that."

He felt the rumble of her laughter and held her close until his erection became all too obvious.

She spoke lazily as he pressed into her. "I should think you'd be tired."

"Tired. Not dead."

She laughed again, and he blessed her when she rolled to her back, tugged him along in her arms, and opened her legs for him. He sank into her, warm and just enough wet, and moved gently. He nibbled at her mouth, taking it slow. "I think I could fall asleep just like this."

She bit back at his lip. "Yeah? Sure. Go ahead."

He moved inside her with a little more intensity. "Well, maybe not *just* like this. Maybe in a few minutes, after..."

"After?"

"After I make you scream. After I come deep inside you."

He did, too. Make her scream. Come deep inside her. Fall asleep just like that.

Sometime later, a pager sounded. He lifted his head, then dropped it back into her shoulder. "Yours or mine?"

"Mine."

"You're not on call again, are you?"

"I am."

"Shit."

"I'm going to need your car."

"Sorry, Sylvie. No one drives my car."

"Remember last night, when you made me leave mine at Marge's house?"

"No one drives my car, Syl."

"Those the keys? On your dresser?"

"Shit. Yeah."

"See you later, stud muffin."

He rolled off her when she poked at him the second or third time. "Yeah, later, baby. Maybe I'll come take another nap on your office couch."

"You can dream."

"I will."

ABOUT THE AUTHOR

Rebecca Skovgaard is a midwife in Rochester, New York. She and her husband are raising (yes, *still)* their three children, who give them great pride. She believes that if you live in Rochester, you can never have too many spring bulbs in the garden or Christmas lights in the trees.

Under the pen name Rachel Billings, she has published several erotic novels.

CPSIA information can be obtained
at www.ICGtesting.com
Printed in the USA
FFOW04n1620230414
4967FF

9 781940 707006